How Far Are You Willing To Go?
Murder Is Just The Beginning

How Far Are You Willing To Go?
Murder Is Just The Beginning

BY

TRACY WILSON

http://beautifulpublications.com

Published by
Beautiful Publications LLC
Stratford, CT 06614

PRINT ISBN: 978-0-98633617-0-8
EBOOK ISBN: 978-0-9863617-1-5

Printed in the United States of America

Dedication

I dedicate this series to myself. This series is my reward for accomplishing what I've always wanted to do.

Thank You

To God for blessing me with the ability, desire, and passion to write.

To my husband and children for being my biggest supporters.

To my dog, Dreyfuss for lying down by my side and keeping me company whether I was working on my book or socializing on-line with my extended family. You were the best dog in the world.

To my mother, Connie Thompson, for always encouraging me to be true to myself.

To my father, Jake Thompson, for sharing my books with the nurses, the hospital staff, and for giving me their feedback. It felt so good to know that you were proud enough of me and my book to tell the world.

To my uncle, Marshall Thompson, for writing your book, giving me a copy of your book, giving everyone a heads up about my books, providing me with future contacts, and for spending the day with me at work. If I didn't know how much you love me and how proud you are of me before, I sure do now! If I can do half the things in my life you've done in your life they'll be no end to the success in store for me!

To Michael Baisden for meeting with me and my husband, listening to me, being honest with me, and taking the time to critique my 1st book.

To Ella Curry, EDC Creations, for the interview, your radio show, and for listing my first book in the top 25.

To Author David L., Total Package Publications, for everything you do to help other authors, for your warped sense of humor, and for never giving up.

To Debra Owsley, Simply Said Reading Accessories, for designing the Beautiful Publications LLC Logo.

To Tiah Short (DC Book Diva), Publishing Demystified, Urban Literary Review for being there when I needed to vent.

To Allison Grace (fullofessence), Peach Dollhouse LLC, for being strong enough to help other authors even when you didn't have strength to help yourself.

To Kenya Nushen for writing from the Marital Position, for always supporting me, and for staying true to who you are.

To my family, friends, and fans for providing me with unconditional support, all your feedback, and for wanting more. This series is for you.

Chapter

1

This *was* the 2nd time I won something from KISS FM! The first time I won something from KISS FM, I won a trip for two to see Luther Vandross and Nancy Wilson in concert at the Crystal Palace in Nassau, Bahamas. I went with my sister and I tried to cram everything I could into that weekend.

My sister doesn't usually drink but when she saw a liquor store with different flavored Bacardi and little sample cups, she couldn't resist trying at least one of them. 11 samples later, we were giggling and chatting with people in the store like we were in the club! It was a little after 11 a.m. – since we had finished our "liquor" breakfast we needed to look for a place to have lunch...but back to the prize I won this time...

I was the 19th caller and my prize was two tickets to Krystals – a club in Jamaica Queens. I was so excited I had to call my best friend Char (short for Charlotte). Char is always there when you need someone to talk to, hang out with, and, even if she's not hungry, if you want her to eat something so you're not eating by yourself, she'll eat again – especially if it's your treat! She'll cut you up in a second – and she can cut through you and break you down to tears with razor sharp words if she feels you need it, but she has a heart of gold and if she has a dollar and you need 50 cents, she'll break that dollar just to help you out.

The phone rang twice before she picked it up...

"Hello?" Char asked as she answered the phone.

"Do you know how to get to Krystals?"

"What's Krystals?"

"It's a club in Jamaica Queens."

"Why you wanna know if I know how to get there?"

"'Cause I just won two tickets from KISS FM for Friday night and I want you to go with me."

"Oh ok – if you find out how to get there, I'll go. Find out if we gotta dress up and let me know."

"Okay – talk to you later."

I called Krystals and asked for directions. I didn't mind that it would take us two hours by subway but I hoped Char wouldn't mind either. The way I saw it, two hours was worth it to get into Krystals for free – especially on Friday night – KISS FM was there live!

When I talked to Char later, she reminded me that it was more than two hours – a lot more – we had to walk from the train then stand outside for about an hour to get in because the line was so long. I didn't even think about how tired we would be when we left, our aching feet, the walk to the train, the ride on the train trying to stay awake, etc., but as luck would have it, after Char reminded me of all this, she still wanted to go! Whew!

When we got to Krystals, as expected, we had a while to wait online while they searched everyone. After about an hour, two gentlemen approached us with a clip board...

"Are you on tonight's guest list?"

"Yes we are – look under Trenice Robertson."

"We don't see you here – are you sure?"

Oh my God! I don't know what I was more afraid of – that we were about to be rejected from the club in front of all these people, or Char. She gave me that look – the one you get when someone's about to, "No-the-fuck-you-did-not-have-me-come down here, stand on line for over an hour," but she didn't! Whew!

3

In that instant, one of the gentlemen said, "Wait here - let me go check the other guest list...."

I was sure everyone could hear me praying out loud, "Lord, please let my name be on that list." Worst case scenario, I would have paid the $30 for us to get in – after 3 hours we were gettin' our groove and drink on!

"Miss Robertson, everything's ok – you and your guest can come on in."

I turned and looked back at the crowd with a' 'yea-that's-right-I'm-on-the-list' smirk - you know damn well they were waitin' for us to be thrown off the line and out the club!

When it came to the search, I got uncomfortable with the quickness. They had a male bodyguard to search the men, and a female bodyguard to search the ladies. Normally this isn't a problem but after I saw how she was pattin' all over this woman in front of me, I knew she wasn't touchin' me...

"Excuse me. Please don't be offended, but I would feel better if he did the search."

She gave a look like, 'what-the-fuck,' but the male body guards smirked at me as if I was flirting with them both and before I could say anything else, one of them grabbed me by the arm, patted me down and said, "Next." Char didn't mind him pattin' her down either.

When we got inside, we looked around for the most important things: the bathroom, the fire exit, the main exit, the bar, and the men. We went into the bathroom and were cordial with the ladies we met in there.

After coming out, I told Char the first round was on me so I proceeded to the bar. After I ordered 2 Bacardi and Coke's, gave the bartender $20 and didn't get back any change, I informed Char that we wouldn't be doing too many rounds!

After we finished our drinks, Char found someone to dance with so I started looking for someone to dance with for myself. Everyone was either dancing with someone or more interested in holding up the wall than dancing so I went into the middle of the floor near Char and her friend and started dancing by myself. A few girls that were sitting at a table decided to get up and join me so I had plenty of company. I had worked up quite a sweat so I sat down to take a break. He sat down beside me.

"Hello."

"Hi." I figured no harm in being cordial.

"You enjoying yourself?"

"Yes."

"I saw you dancing earlier."

"You wanna dance?" I just assumed this is where he was leading but you know what happens when you assume right?

"No - I don't dance. I came with a friend of mine and he's dancing so I'm just gonna sit."

I shrugged my shoulders as if to say, "Oh well," and got up to go sit somewhere else.

"Where you goin'?"

This kinda surprised me 'cause I really didn't think he was the least bit interested but I didn't feel the need to be rude so I said, "I'm here with my best friend – I wanna see where she's at."

"Oh ok – come back when you find her."

"Ok I will. Hmm," I thought.

I found Char and pointed him out at the table so she would see where I was at. He was all smiles. I went back to the table and sat down.

"I didn't think you would come back."

"Well, you thought wrong I guess."

We both laughed then he got to the point...

"Are you seeing anyone right now?"

Usually I would say yes when this happened 'cause it was true or I wasn't interested and I didn't want to hurt the guy's feelings, but this time it wasn't either. My answer; however, was just as disappointing.

"No, but I'm pursuing someone right now."

"Pursuing someone?" He had a perplexed look on his face so I figured I might as well tell him the truth. I don't know why I felt so comfortable with him but the perplexed look on his face was so sad and familiar, I felt I had to explain. I wasn't sure what difference it would make, but I couldn't just leave it like that so I proceeded to tell him all about Tony...

"I met Tony after I moved in with my grandmother. I was coming into the building with my groceries and he held the door for me. That was unusual – usually the guys would hurry past you and let the door close in your face. After holding the door for me, he helped me with my groceries to my door – that's when I found out we were neighbors and he lived with his grandmother too.

Tony was different from other guys in the complex – he was kinda shy in a way. You never saw him drinking a forty outside, being loud like the rest of them. He would get his smoke on though, but if you were asleep, he didn't wake you up with loud-ass noise under your window. He was respectful to the ladies in the complex – he held door for them, helped them with their groceries, helped them with their carriages, and he would even offer to call you a taxi if you were waiting and cussin 'cause they told you 5 minutes and it had been 20 minutes. Whenever I saw him I would always say, "Hello Tony," and his friends would mock me in unison, "Hello Tony." This went on for two weeks. When I would see him outside alone, I would sit next to him and we would talk about our day at work, the weather, TV shows, etc, until his friends came along and said in unison, "Hello Tony." Sadly, he would get up and tell me, "Well, I guess I'll see you later," and he would go inside.

One night I saw Tony outside and I sat down to talk with him. We were having a good conversation and I was about to tell him how I felt about him but, like clockwork, here come his friends, mocking me in unison, "Hello Tony." When he got up to leave, I gently tugged his arm and said, "It's nice out and it's Friday night. Let's stay outside for a while." As happy as I was that he sat back down, I was so mad that his friends decided to sit down and join us. I was determined to tell him how I felt, even if it meant waiting all night until his friends went inside. After about ½ hour, his friends went inside and we were alone – finally!

"I really like you Tony."

"I really like you too Trenice."

"I was beginning to wonder about that – every time your friends came around, you left."

"I wanted to tell you how I felt, but I was afraid of what you would say."

"Tony, I need your help in the kitchen...."

"Shit!" I said to myself. "Just when we were gettin' somewhere..."

"Well, I better go inside, I'll see ya later."

"I'd seen Tony a couple of times since then and he would always say hello, hold the door for me, and help me with my groceries, but we haven't spoken about that night since."

I couldn't believe it. I had just spilled out my guts to a complete stranger. I don't know why

I did or why he listened. Why did he listen? He gave me his undivided attention the whole time.

After a few minutes of silence he said, "Don't get me wrong, but hasn't he taken up enough of your time? He had his chance – he blew it – now it's my turn."

"Your turn?"

"Yes. I've seen you before and I wanted to talk to you but I thought you were involved. I couldn't believe my luck when I saw you in here tonight. When you pointed me out and came back to the table, I knew I had to talk to you tonight. Lets go someplace where we can talk some more. Why don't you tell your friend you're going with me? I'll make sure you get home."

Hold up! I wanted to go with him. It had been a long time since I enjoyed myself like this. I felt like I could talk with him forever. I trusted him. But Char and I had a rule: we go out together, we go home together. Period. As bad as I wanted to go with him, the other voice in my head started yelling at me...

"Are you crazy? You don't even know his name! You don't know anything about him!"

My other voice said, "There's something about him... you can trust him, this feels right..."

"Trenice I'm ready," Char said, interrupting my thoughts.

"Char this is...by the way, what is your name?" "Jordan." I liked that...

"Char, Jordan has invited me to go with him and he'll make sure I get home."

Char's eyes popped out her head and she opened her mouth to cut me down, but I was one up on both of them – before she could say a word I said, "They take pictures right?"

"Why?" Jordan looked perplexed too – good!

"Well, he can take a picture of us and I'll give it to you. If you don't hear from me by tomorrow afternoon, you can give it to the police and tell them, "This is the person she left with."

Char's eyes got wide again, but she had a big smile on her face. She taught me well. Whenever she met someone she would call me and give me the digits, the address, and the license plate to the car. If I didn't hear from her within 24 hours, I was to call the police. She even told them, "My best friend has your digits, your address, and your license plate and if she doesn't hear from me in the morning, she's going to the police." Thank God I always heard from her.

Jordan smiled to himself and when we posed for the picture, he snuck up behind me, placed his arm around my waist, and gently pulled me close to him. "Take two," he said. The 1st picture he gave to Char. "You can give this back to Trenice later." The 2nd picture he put in his pocket.

"Can we drop Char off and then go where ever we're going?"

"Sure." We went outside to the car and got in.

"Do you have a driver's license?"

"Of course."

"May I see it?"

"Sure."

I took one look at his driver's license and bust out laughing. Jordan seemed annoyed but didn't say anything. I passed it to Char and she took one look at it and bust out laughing.

Jordan looked back at Char, looked at me, and said in a somewhat annoyed tone, "So where to Char?"

"Across the street from you."

We all bust out laughing.

Chapter 2

Jordan and I spent the wee hours of the morning at the movies! After leaving Yonkers, we drove all the way back to New York City and found an all night theatre on 42nd Street. They were running Star Wars, The Empire Strikes Back, and Return of the Jedi back to back for the price of 1 movie. I loved the Star Wars movies – this was great!

We got out the movies at 7 a.m. I was dead-tired, but I didn't want to go home. "I'm tired but I don't wanna go home yet."

"So let's not go home then." We went to IHOP for breakfast. I had pancakes with blueberries and Jordan had pancakes with strawberries. We also had fruit salad, scrambled eggs with cheese, turkey sausage, and coffee. It was 9 a.m. when we finally asked the waitress for the check. She seemed a bit annoyed but when Jordan gave her a $20 tip, she was happy indeed.

As we talked on the way home, I found out that Jordan's grandmother and my grandmother knew each other and they were good friends. My grandmother always talked about her good friend April but who'd a thought? I lived with my grandmother, Jordan lived with his grandmother, and they were good friends. Just when I started feeling really high on life, Jordan leaned over and kissed me on the cheek. When he got out and opened the door for me I thought, "Oh God – I hope were not related...."

"You slept with him didn't you?"

"No Grandma."

"Yes you did."

"No I didn't Grandma – I would tell you if I did."

And I would have too. Grandma was cool that way. She made us feel comfortable from early on – whatever we wanted to tell her we could. We had to be prepared for the consequences but she had our back and she believed it was better for us to come to her before something happened so she could prevent it. Whenever you went to Grandma she would call Mom and say, "What did you do to this child this time?" Whatever you told Grandma stayed with Grandma – or so I thought...

Chapter 3

It was 1 pm when I called Char. "Girl, I was comin' over there to tell Grandma. So how was it?"

"Char, he's wonderful! We went to the movies then breakfast. You know Grandma had to grill me when I came in right?"

"Well did you?"

"No."

"Trenice, you left here at 2 a.m. this morning. Its 1 p.m. in the afternoon. You just gettin' home and all you did was go to the movies and breakfast? You think I'm stupid?"

I couldn't believe she asked me that. As long as we've known each other we always gave each other the 411 on the dick – the good, the bad, the long, the short, the thin, and the thick of it. "Char, as long as we've know each other…"

"You're right Trenice – I'm sorry. So did it look like he has a big dick?"

We bust out laughing.

Chapter

4

I called Jordan at 10 a.m. on Sunday. When I got off the phone at 2 p.m. Grandma said, "Whad ya do – tell him your life story? That's the longest you've ever been on the phone!"

I was on cloud 9 for the rest of the day. I couldn't believe we talked for so long – I don't even remember half of what we said – all I knew was I didn't want the conversation to end. His voice was soothing and comforting and I was beginning to realize that Jordan was giving me something that had been missing in my life for a long time. I enjoyed being alone but I was tired of being lonely. Besides, it had been 6 months since I broke things off for good with Torbett and

I needed to move on. I needed everything Jordan could provide intellectually, psychologically, emotionally, physically, and sexually.

It had been 6 months since I broke it off with Torbett but it was over between us long before then. In the beginning of our relationship Torbett and I were inseparable. I had met him in my senior year of high school. Once I graduated from high school, Torbett and I moved in together. We lived together for about a year and things were fine until Torbett lost his job.

I was working but it wasn't enough. It didn't take long for Torbett to lose his temper. He would fly off the handle whenever he came in after 2 a.m. smelling like liquor and I asked where he was all day. Losing his job and his temper wasn't enough – that damn fool lost his mind when he slapped me for questioning him. I was smart enough to know that at 6 foot 10, 300 pounds he would break my ass in half if I slapped him back, but I was even smarter to leave his ass!

"Trenice, please don't leave – it'll never happen again..."

"I know that's right," I said as I walked out the door and headed straight to Grandma's house.

Grandma never liked Torbett. "There's something about him..." she always said. But she never butt in when Torbett came over and talked me into giving him another chance.

Everything was ok for a while. Torbett had gotten himself a good job and he had cut down on the drinking considerably. We met each other on Fridays, we got a room for the weekend, and I was back at Grandma's house on Sunday night. After a month, Torbett started coming to pick me up every other weekend. It seems he was working overtime so he couldn't pick me up every weekend like before. After two months of this, it was once a month. That voice went off in my head, "What are you doing? You deserve a lot more than this."

I picked up the phone as Grandma was on her way into the kitchen to make coffee. "Hello? Torbett?"

"Yes?"

"It's over. If you have anything to say, don't bother. I don't want to hear it. Don't come by to see me. I have nothing else to say to you after this. If you send any letters, I'll return them unopened. First we were seeing each other once a week. Then twice a month. Then once a month. Now we're not seeing each other at all. Goodbye."

"Okay." Dial tone.

That was all he had to say. That told me I did the right thing. Grandma came out of the kitchen sipping her coffee. She looked at me and smiled without saying a word. I met Tony the following week and that brings us back to Jordan.

Chapter 5

Jordan came over to Grandma's house a week later to meet her. It was Father's Day, June 15th. Grandma liked him immediately. I listened intently as she told Jordan stories about how she was the bartender at the Black Horse, which Jordan's grandmother owned. She laughed and continued to talk about how she and his grandmother would help the bouncers throw people out of the bar when they had too much liquor and she and his grandmother would go clubin' together on their days off.

When Jordan asked if she ever met his father she said, "Yea, I knew him," then she changed the subject. "So where are you and

Trenice off too?" I wondered why she did such an about face but I didn't worry about us being related anymore 'cause Grandma would've told me from jump if she thought I had anything to worry about.

"We're going downtown to the movies and dinner." I already knew where we were going and I couldn't wait to leave and spend the day with him.

We spent the day in the city. We went to central park, the movies, and Tad's Steakhouse for dinner. When Jordan brought me home, Aunt Trudy was all in it...

"Hi Trenice – who's this?"

"Hi Aunt Trudy – this is Jordan."

"Where'd you meet?"

"We met at Krystals."

"How long y'all been going out?"

"Two weeks."

"Oh that's nice – alright Ma ‑ I'll see you later – nice meeting you Jordan," she said as she left.

"Well I better get going – I gotta get up early for work tomorrow – let me say good night to your grandmother."

That was the highlight of my day! Torbett had never done that unless my grandmother was in the living room when we got home. "Grandma, can you come out here? Jordan wants to say good night." I guess that was the highlight of her day too 'cause she came out grinning from ear to ear.

"Good night Miss Gladys."

"Good night Jordan."

He gave me a kiss on the cheek and went out the door.

"Sit down and tell me about your day."

"Well Grandma, it was great..." I was interrupted by a knock on the door.

"Who?"

"Trudy."

I opened the door and let her in.

"Trenice was just gettin' ready to tell me about her date."

"Ma, he's married. His wife's name is Rosalind and I work with her at the hospital. I saw Jordan come take her to lunch the other day."

"Are you sure Trudy?"

"I'm sure Ma."

"Don't tell him I told you Trenice – just break it off now."

"Okay I will," I lied. "Oh no the hell he didn't," I thought to myself.

"All right Ma – I'll see ya later."

"All right Trudy." Soon as the door closed she asked, "What are you gonna do?"

"I'm gonna tell him what Aunt Trudy said tomorrow Grandma."

Chapter
6

Jordan came to pick me up Monday night. I waited for him outside in front of the building purposely because I wanted to question him without my grandmother and Aunt Trudy in his face. He must have been running late because I had been waiting an hour already.

"You've been waiting a long time."

I turned around and who was standing there but Tony!

"Yea I have been." All I could think was, "Oh now you wanna talk to me," but I bit my lip.

"I would never keep you waiting this long."

I wanted to tell him, "Mothafucka he's only kept me waiting an hour – you kept me waiting for a couple of weeks!" but I bit my lip again.

"I'm sure he's on his way."

"You look cold – here take my jacket."

"Thanks."

"I'll sit here and keep you company but if he's not here in another ½ hour, you should go back upstairs."

I wanted Jordan so bad just then. I just wanted to save face. I don't know why I cared what Tony thought but I did. Just as I started gettin' anxious Jordan came flying around the corner...

"Sorry I'm late – I had to help Grandma. You still wanna go? If you're mad I'll understand." Mad was the last thing I was.

"Thanks for the jacket Tony," I said as I gave it back to him.

"I'm Jordan – nice to meet you – good lookin' out," he said as he shook Tony's hand.

When we walked around the corner I stopped at a stoop and sat down. "We need to talk Jordan – sit down."

"What's wrong?"

"Remember when you came to Grandma's house and met my Aunt Trudy?"

"Yea."

"Well, she says you're married. She says your wife's name is Rosalind and she works at the hospital with her. She also said you came to pick her up for lunch one day last week."

I watched the expression on Jordan's face change. He was sad, but then he got quite angry. "Rosalind is my ex-wife. We got a divorce 6 months ago. I was at the hospital last week to drop off some papers. I was gonna tell you tonight. You still wanna go out?"

"Yea."

"Okay let's go then."

We went to the city, to central park, to the movies, and out to dinner. I had a good time but I could tell Jordan was preoccupied. That was understandable. We didn't talk much – we just walked hand in hand or arm in arm.

I decided to give him the benefit of the doubt and trust him. When he brought me back home Grandma had her own agenda.

"Sit down Jordan." Oh boy. Here it comes.

"Grandma, Jordan..."

"Shut up Trenice!" I sat down and shut up quick.

"I heard you were married – is that true?"

"Yes. Rosalind is my ex-wife. We've been divorced for 6 months. I told Trenice tonight."

"Well if you wanna see my granddaughter again, I better see some divorce papers. Good night."

Grandma beat me to the punch. I had every intention of asking to see those papers but she told me to shut up so I didn't open my mouth.

"Good night Miss Gladys." He kissed me on the cheek and closed the door behind him.

I didn't hear from Jordan for over a week. Grandma didn't say anything about it either. Thank God she didn't 'cause I don't know what I would have said.

The following Saturday there was a knock at the door. Grandma was in the kitchen making us coffee...

"Who?"

"Jordan." I was so happy I ran to the door, opened it, and went to throw my arms around him but he pushed me back.

"I need to see your grandmother."

"Come on in Jordan," she said as she sat our coffee on the table and I noticed Jordan was carrying a metal box. We sat at the table and Jordan pulled up a chair and scooted between Grandma and me.

"I have something to show you Miss Gladys," he said as he pulled out a bunch of papers and spread them out on the table. Grandma went over each paper as if it were a contract she had to sign. Jordan had a very serious look on his face. I was so happy I wanted to cry, but I fought back tears. Jordan sat back and watched as Grandma went through the divorce papers.

"Ok Jordan, you can put these away now."

"So I have permission to see your granddaughter?"

"You have my permission," she said.

Jordan went to pick up all of the papers to put them back in the metal box but I snatched them up before he could. I turned to the last page. The divorce was granted about 6 ½ months ago.

Tuesday night Aunt Trudy came over again. "Hi Ma, hi Trenice. What happened with you and Jordan?"

"Oh we're fine."

"But I told you he was married."

"But I saw his divorce papers," Grandma yelled from her bedroom.

I heard a knock on the door, but Aunt Trudy beat me to it..."Hi Jordan," she said slyly as she opened the door.

I was waiting for him to say, "Don't fuckin' speak to me," but instead he said, "Hello Trudy – Trenice you ready?"

"Yea."

"See you later Trudy – bye Miss Gladys."

"Bye Jordan," Grandma yelled from her room.

When we got out into the hallway, Jordan kissed me on the lips for the first time. Finally! After 4 weeks, I finally got to taste those lips! "I love you," he said as he pulled me in close to him again and began to explore my mouth with his tongue. This went straight to my clit and once my panties got wet, I knew I was in trouble...

"We better get going before someone comes into the hallway," I said between kisses...

"Yea we better," he said as we continued kissing for a few minutes. As bad as I wanted him we had a lot more to talk about before I took that step.

Chapter 7

I knew after the movies and dinner we would need to talk. I had planned to wait until tomorrow but Jordan wasn't waiting until then. To tell the truth, neither was I. Kissing me in my mouth opened a gusher and it needed to erupt! I had to get this situation back under control – and I had to do it quick. Don't get me wrong – my panties weren't wet for nothing. You can go for weeks without the dick and all of a sudden, out of nowhere, bam! The pussy's cravin' dick like an addict craves crack and a dildo just won't do!

We were at Tad's Steakhouse and we had already ordered. We had a cozy table in the corner in the back. The lights were dimmed so it looked like we were eating by candlelight. "It's now or never," I thought...

"So how'd you like it?" Jordan asked as he interrupted my thoughts.

"The movie? Oh it was good..." I knew damn well he wasn't talking about the movie.

He smiled at me and said, "How'd you like the kiss?"

"Oh that." I leaned across the table, pulled his face to mine and kissed him lightly at first, then I began to kiss him harder and explore his mouth with my tongue the same way he explored mine earlier....

"Ahem!" We both looked up and there was the waiter with our steaks and salads. "Will there be anything else?"

"Not right now, but if we change our mind, we'll call you," I said. Boy I'm gonna have to wring these panties out when I get home...

"That was nice," Jordan said.

"Yes it was – but we need to talk."

"What's wrong?"

"Nothing – nothing at all but..."

"Are you sure everything's ok?"

"Let me finish."

"Ok."

"Before I met Torbett I was in a relationship with Nathaniel. I really loved him and I thought he really loved me too. He used to tell me I was his number 1 lady. One day his twin brother, Daniel, sat me down to explain what that meant. Nathaniel did love me and I was his number 1 lady – but Chelly was number 2, Tonya was number 3, Vicki was number 4 etc. I couldn't deal with that because I'm extremely selfish and possessive when it comes to my man – I don't want to share him with anyone – I want him all to myself – it's not enough for me to be number 1 – I have to be the only one. I give as good as I get – if you give me 100% I'll give you 110%. If this is a problem for you or if you're seeing other people let me know right now so we can go our separate ways."

I waited for Jordan to say something but he didn't. He just looked at me for about a minute without blinking.

"Are you ok?"

"Yea – it's just that I've never been told that before." He then proceeded to tell me about his ex-wife.

"I really loved Rosalind. We were married two years after we met. I really loved her. Even after I found out she was seeing someone else while we were married, I stayed with her for a while to try and work it out. When she told me she was pregnant I was ecstatic but she told me she wasn't ready for a baby. She had an abortion without telling me. That really hurt but I stayed with her for a while anyway. I just couldn't let go until she gave me no choice. When she got pregnant the 2nd time she put the knife in my back and twisted it. She told me it was Steven's baby and she wanted to end our marriage and be with him."

I saw tears in Jordan's eyes for the first time. I took his left hand and placed it gently in mine. The waiter came over and when he saw the tears in Jordan's eyes he turned and walked away.

We didn't say anything else while we finished our dinner. We walked to the subway hand in hand or arm in arm. The whole ride home we just sat next to each other holding each other. When we got home he kissed me passionately. "I love you. Good night."

I stood at the door and watched him walk downstairs.

I couldn't sleep. It was 2 a.m. Wednesday morning. I heard Grandma put the chain on the door like she always does once she knows I'm in for the night. As she walked down the hallway I smelled her coffee and I wanted some so I got up and made myself a cup. I sat at the kitchen table and wrote Jordan this poem:

I Can't Believe I'm In Love

You changed my life when you came in my world,
Now I'm glad that I'm your girl.
I Can't Believe – I Can't Believe I'm In Love.

Lonely my sickness – you're my cure.
I want this feeling forever more.
I Can't Believe – I Can't Believe I'm In Love.

Deep inside I know it's not infatuation.
When you hold me tight I can feel good
vibrations.
I just want you to be mine until the end of time

God has answered my every prayer.
He sent someone who really cares.
I Can't Believe – I Can't Believe I'm In Love.

Chapter
8

I was dead tired. It was 3 p.m. and I was comin' down. Good thing I had a lot to do 'cause I'd be asleep at this desk. All I could think about was stopping by Jordan's house after work. I was nervous about giving him the poem I wrote. What would he think of it? Would he like it? Would he think I was silly? Would he think I was immature? 4:45 p.m. – shit I gotta go! I punched out and ran to Jordan's house.

When I got there I knocked on the door. "May I help you?"

"I'm Trenice – is Jordan home?"

"He's not here – you wanna wait for him?"

"Sure."

"You look familiar – what's your mother's name?"

"Claire."

"Claire's your mother? You look just like her! I've known your mother and grandmother for years!"

"You're Miss April?" I asked.

"Yes – I'm Jordan's grandmother and this is his mother, June."

"Nice meeting you both." Just then, Jordan came in the door.

"Hey Mum-Mum – hey Trenice – whatchu doin' here?"

"I have something for you."

Let me change and then we can go outside." This took all but two minutes.

When we got downstairs, we saw Char. "Hi Trenice, hi Jordan!" she yelled as she drove past.

"So what you got for me?" he asked.

"Let's go somewhere and sit down." I said.

We walked to the park in the next block and found a bench off by itself. We sat down and I handed him my poem. He read the poem, put it back in his pocket and said, "It's nice." He took my hand and led me to the tree in the middle of the grass. When we sat down he slid up behind me, wrapped his arm around me and pulled me close to him. We stayed like that in the park and I fell asleep. Jordan woke me up at 8 p.m. and said, "I think I better get you home."

I got up Thursday morning and got ready for work as usual, but I was unusually quiet.

"What's your problem?" Grandma said.

"Nothing."

"Don't give me that nothing shit – what's wrong?"

"Nothing Grandma – really."

"Let me see your eyes...they mighty red – you been smoking that shit?"

"No Grandma – I'm just tired. There's nothing wrong – I swear."

"Well you better not be smoking that shit!"

"Grandma – you know I can't lie to you," I laughed. I was telling the truth on both counts. I wasn't smoking that shit and you couldn't lie to Grandma. She could see right through you - so don't even try it.

She smiled at me and said, "I know you don't lie to me."

"Have a good day," I said as I kissed her cheek and went off to work.

I got off work at 5 p.m. and Jordan was there waiting for me. "Let's go," he said as he took my hand.

"Where we goin'?" I asked as he pulled me across the street.

"Come with me," he said.

We went back to the park and sat down on the bench. Jordan took out a radio cassette player and popped in a tape. I cried as I listened to him singing to me the poem I wrote to him, which he put to his music. We went to a studio that weekend, had a demo made, and had our song copy-written.

The following week I was at Jordan's house every night after work. Miss June would stay in the bedroom and Miss April would come back and forth listening to us singing to the music we were playin' and listen to us singing to music we were makin'. Sometimes we got carried away and she'd yell, "People tryin' to sleep and it's gettin' late!" That was usually are cue to pack it in.

I remember the first time I sang for Jordan. I was nervous as hell. I had been singing in church and in chorus but I was afraid Jordan would tell me I couldn't sing. Nothing was further from the truth. Once he heard me sing he wanted me to sing all the time.

We spent every night at his house putting songs to music. Jordan was really impressed with my songs and my writing ability. He would often make comments like, "great analogy," or "nice change." I heard many of his songs and I picked out my favorites. In fact, my brother Marlowe would come downstairs (my mother, brothers, and sisters lived upstairs on the 4th floor and Jordan, his mother, and his grandmother lived on the 2nd floor) and he couldn't remember the name of the song he liked that Jordan wrote but he would ask, "Can I hear that song again?" The song was, 'Foolish Guy' and Jordan was always happy to play it for him.

I loved Jordan's voice too. I found out that he had been in a band in the 70's, 'Heat, Energy, & Mass' but the name was quickly changed to 'Stone.' Thomas Blidge, Mary J. Blidge's father, was the bass player and Jimmy Miller, Mary J. Blidge's uncle, was the guitar player. Jordan was nicknamed 'Gino-Smokey Robinson' because his voice was very similar to Smokey Robinson's voice. Jordan also performed Smokey Robinson's song, 'Tell Me Tomorrow' at Trevor Park in Yonkers every year when they had the African American Heritage Festival.

We also spent a lot of weekends at Cain's house in School Street where we sang with Arnette, DMX's mother. When I met William, the first thing I noticed was his strong resemblance to Lionel Richie. William had a voice that was better than Lionel Richie's – he could sing Lionel's songs but he could also hit notes higher than Philip Bailey, the lead singer of Earth, Wind, & Fire. William was also a songwriter and Jordan arranged his music on the song, 'Tonight,' and he co-wrote a song with William entitled, 'Never Thought.' I loved to hear William and Jordan sing together and whenever they needed a background singer, I was more than happy to volunteer.

Chapter 9

Jordan came to pick me up at 12 p.m. Saturday. I was wondering who was with him. When he came on the porch he introduced us.

"Jake, this is Trenice – Trenice, this is my best friend Jake and his lady Rachel. They're gonna chill with us today – do you mind?"

"No – I don't mind." To be honest I wasn't sure but what was I gonna say?

We went to the bus stop and caught the bus to the subway. We laughed and talked on the subway and got to know each other. Jordan seemed really happy that we got along so well.

We went to central park, the movies, and dinner. Before we left the restaurant, Rachel and I got up to go to the ladies room.

"So you like Jordan?" she asked me as she was fixin' her hair.

"Like him? I don't just like him – I love him." That was the first time I told anyone other than Jordan that I loved him.

We went back to the table and had dessert. After dessert we left the restaurant and went back to central park. We watched the sun go down and once it started to get chilly Rachel said, "Jake I'm ready to go."

"Why we gotta leave so soon?" Jake asked her.

"Cause I'm ready," she said in a seductive voice."

Jordan and I looked at them and then at each other. We were 'ready' too.

Chapter
10

Early Sunday morning Jordan came to pick me up for breakfast. I was waiting downstairs so I wouldn't wake up anyone in the house. There were only a few people out and I loved the peace and quiet. Jordan come up on the porch and kissed me hello. We went to the bus stop and once we were on the bus I was deep in thought.

"Why you so quiet?"

"Just thinking."

"Something good I hope?"

"Very." If he could have read my mind at that moment, let alone see the pictures in my mind...

We rode the subway to 42nd Street and went straight for breakfast. We went back to IHOP and started out with coffee and juice, then graduated to fruit, cheddar omelets, corn muffins, turkey sausage then refills on the coffee. It's a good thing Jordan spoke first 'cause I didn't know where to begin.

"So do you make a lot of noise?"

"Huh?" I said as he interrupted my day dream...

"During sex, do you make a lot of noise?"

"No. I don't think you need to advertise what you're doing. I'm not saying I don't make any noise, but all that loud noise isn't necessary. If it's natural and you're enjoying it then fine but I don't think most women do all that screaming and carrying on."

"Oh. Well I make noise," he said.

"Oh I see."

"Do you like oral sex?"

"It depends."

"On what?" he asked as he leaned across the table, anxious to hear what I was going to say next...

"Well, I don't think there's anything wrong with it but I do think it's something sacred. I don't think that should be done with just anyone – I think that should be between two people who really care about each other. I also think if a woman enjoys giving her man pleasure that she shouldn't be looked at as a whore or a slut and she should be able to please her man and herself if she chooses without it being thrown back in her face." I should have stopped there but I was on a roll..."When I was with Torbett, he would always go back and run his mouth when we had sex and he would make comments like, "your pussy was yappin," in front of his friends. He didn't believe in oral sex either and as far as he was concerned, if a woman sucked dick she was a whore so I never brought it up. Little did he know that whenever we finished having sex, I'd end up going in the bathroom to finish what he started!" Oh boy! I really went too far this time! Why didn't I quit while I was ahead? Why did I tell him that? Oh well fuck it – it's out now – he knows.

"I'm sorry," Jordan said.

"For what?"

"You seem upset – I didn't mean to upset you."

"You didn't upset me – I just got caught up in an old moment," I laughed.

"I hate when guys do that shit. It's one thing if you're sittin' with the guys but you should never disrespect your lady like that."

"I love making love and I want to feel comfortable enough to do things and explore with my man. I don't want to have to worry about if he'll think I'm a whore because I want to try something different. For me it's not just the dick. I want my man to make love to me but I want to make love to him as well. I want to be able to love his whole body from head to toe, rub his back and his shoulders, kiss the small of his back and his ass, suck his toes, and if I choose to suck his dick, the only pussy I want to taste is mine!" I didn't realize I had raised my voice but the stares and smiles I got let me know rather quickly. Normally I would have been embarrassed, but I just looked at Jordan and smiled.

"You don't have to worry about any of that with me. I'm not intimidated by an aggressive woman – I love it when a woman wants to take charge – and you don't have to worry about gettin' pregnant – I believe in condoms."

"I don't like condoms."

"What?"

"Some of them leave me chafed and besides – I want to feel you inside me – not a condom."

"You want to feel me inside you?"

I hadn't realized I said that until he repeated it.

"Yes indeed."

"What if you get pregnant?"

"I won't get pregnant 'cause I use birth control – and neither of us will catch anything 'cause we'll both go to the doctor and get tested before we make love."

"Sounds like a plan."

When we got home I had to call Char.

"Hello?"

"I'm comin' over," I said.

"Ok – I'll meet you downstairs."

When I got to Char's house I gave her the 411 on our conversation.

"Oh my God – what did he say?"

"Well, he said he makes noise, he likes aggressive women, and it sounds like a plan."

"Girl, I can't wait for this – when you finally get it you gotta give me the details!"

Chapter 11

Jordan and I made an appointment for the following Monday. We agreed we would use the same doctor and that we would both be in the room when the doctor read us our results.

The doctor was pleasantly surprised. "I wish more of my patients did what you two are doing. It would save them all so much grief."

We were both given clean bills of health as far as the GYN exams, but we were told we would receive the results of the blood test in the mail in about two weeks.

I smiled to myself as we left the doctor's office. Jordan and I were the only ones who knew what went on in that bathroom. He went in first to give his urine sample and when I went in I told him, "Wait here." I heard someone try to come in and I heard him say, "Someone's in here," so they must have gone to sit back down. When I was finished I pulled Jordan into the bathroom and locked the door.

"Trenice, what are you doing?"

"I want you to be the first one inside me – not the doctor," I said as I took his hand and guided it underneath my skirt. I had removed my panties so Jordan knew exactly what I wanted him to do. He pulled me close to him with his other hand, kissed me, and we began exploring each other's mouths with our tongues as he slid two fingers inside my pussy. I placed my hand down his pants and grabbed his cock as we continued to explore each other's mouths and bodies. We were interrupted by a knock on the door so we quickly adjusted ourselves and went into the waiting room. The other patients were smiling at us but the lab tech that needed to remove the urine samples from the bathroom looked at us in disgust...

Chapter 12

"You little freak! I can't believe you did that shit! You go Girl," Char said as we both bust out laughing. "So you had his dick in your hand right?"

"Oh yea!"

"How was it?"

"Whatchu mean?"

"I know it was hard – is it big?"

"I loved the feel of his dick in my hand. It was hard, thick, and smooth."

"Did you get to see it?"

"No I was just feelin' it and imagining what it would feel like inside me girl."

"I hear that – so do you think he eats pussy?"

"Well the way we were talking a couple a days ago he probably does. I told him about Torbett and Torbett didn't believe in that shit remember?"

"Oh yea – you did tell me that..."

"Well, Jordan didn't say he ate pussy but he didn't say he didn't either."

"Oh girl you good to go then."

"I sure hope so. I've never had that done to me before so he'll be my first."

"Get the fuck outta here! Never?"

"Never."

"Ain't this about a bitch – you an oral virgin!" We hollered on that one.

"I hope he's the first man to make me cum too."

"Watchu mean the first man to make you cum? You don't cum?"

"Oh I cum all the time – it'll just be nice to have a man make me cum for a change. I told him when I was with Torbett I usually had to go in the bathroom to finish what he started."

"That's right – you did tell me that – I guess he wasn't shit in bed huh?"

"He could light the match – he just couldn't fan the flames!"

We bust out laughing again.

Chapter 13

I had been takin these fuckin' pills for two weeks and I was already sick of 'em – literally…"Ugh!"

"What's wrong with you girl?"

"Nothing Grandma – I'm just nauseous."

"What you got the flu?"

"I hope not Grandma." When I came out the bathroom she corned me.

"What's going on Trenice?"

"Nothing Grandma."

"Come sit down." Oh boy – here it comes…

"You want some coffee Trenice?"

"Yea Grandma – sit down – I'll make it." I figured I might as well tell Grandma 'cause she was gonna push the issue anyway. I put two cups of coffee on the table and sat down.

"You love him don't you?"

"Yes Grandma – very much."

"Your Aunt Trudy says you're pregnant. She saw you runnin' to the bathroom the other day. Are you?"

"No Grandma."

"You sure? Don't let me find out you lyin' to me..."

"Grandma you know I never lie to you."

"I know you never lie to me but I also know you're keeping something from me. Don't do like my daughters did – they told me after they were 5 months pregnant so I couldn't do anything about it. If you're pregnant just tell me – you know I love you no matter what and you also know you ain't ready for no baby."

I love my grandmother but I didn't want to tell her. Aunt Trudy had already seen me running to the bathroom. They probably talked about me and if Aunt Trudy asked her, she would tell her and Aunt Trudy has a big fuckin' mouth – I don't need the United States knowing my business. But I saw how Grandma was looking at me. I knew she loved me and I didn't want to hurt her – and I could see this was hurting her so I figured what the hell...

"Grandma?"

"Yes?"

"You know I been sick..."

"Yea? So?"

"It's from the pill."

"What pill?" I almost didn't want to answer her 'cause she had that 'bitch-don't-make-me-slap-you look on her face.

"Birth control pills. I'm on birth control Grandma." I waited for the 'you aint married lecture' but instead I got a big hug.

"Thank God you had the good sense to realize you ain't ready for no baby."

"I know Grandma. Me and Jordan went to the doctor last month to get checked and for me to start the pill."

"Hold it – get checked? He got something?"

"No Grandma – we just went together – I went for him and he went for me."

"Well you need to go back to the doctor and change those pills – you shouldn't be sick like that. If you had told me sooner I would have told you."

"I didn't know Grandma – I never used the pill before."

"You didn't? What about Torbett?"

"Oh I didn't have to worry about him Grandma – he's sterile."

I went to the doctor and told her about my 'morning, noon, and night sickness.' She changed my prescription and I took them in the evenings instead of the morning. As usual, Grandma knew what she was talking about.

When I got back home I ran smack into Sissy – Aunt Trudy's girlfriend. I can't stand that nosy bitch.

"Are you or ain't ya?" she yelled to the whole fuckin' neighborhood. I kept walking like I didn't hear her. Fuckin' nosy bitch!

Chapter 14

I got my blood test results in the mail on Monday. I knew they would be negative but I opened them and read them anyway. "Negative," I said. Just like I thought." Just then I got a wonderful idea.

I called the Holiday Inn Crowne Plaza in White Plains. "Holiday Inn may I help you?"

"I'd like to book a room for Sunday night."

"Single?"

"Yes single."

"What credit card would you like to use?" "MasterCard."

I booked the room at the Holiday Inn Crowne Plaza in White Plains 'cause I didn't want to run into anybody in Yonkers – especially if I was going to a hotel with Jordan. I was so excited I ran to the bathroom to shower and get dressed…

"Shit, Dammit, Motherfucker!" I yelled.

"Trenice you alright?"

"Yea I'm ok Grandma – I hit my toe on the toilet." I couldn't tell Grandma the real reason I was cussin'. I couldn't tell Grandma I had just booked a room for Sunday night so I could get some dick and I just got my fuckin' period! I started thinking …"Wait a minute! Today's Monday! My period should be gone by Saturday!" I came out the bathroom smiling like the cat that swallowed the canary. I got dressed, went downstairs, and high-tailed it to Jordan's job. When I saw him I went flyin' across the store…

"Something wrong?"

"I got it."

"What?"

"The test results – did you get yours?"

"Wait here." I saw him go talk to someone – I guess it was his supervisor. "C'mon let's go home and check my mail."

We flew out the store to his house.

"Hi Mum-Mum did I get any mail?"

"Here – Hi Trenice."

"Hi Miss April – Hi Miss June."

"Jordan smiled to himself as he read the results then passed me the paper so I could read them. I read the results, took out my paper and gave it to him so he could read mine. He read the results, pulled me close and kissed me so hard I almost 'came' on myself.

"I better get back to work…"

"Yea you better."

"Bye Mum-Mum."

"Bye Miss April – bye Miss June."

While we were walking back to his Job I told Jordan I had booked a room for Sunday at the Holiday Inn Crowne Plaza in White Plains. "See you Sunday," he said as he gave me a kiss.

"See you Sunday," I said as I headed back towards Grandma's house.

"Girl, you gonna git it now," Char said when I called her and told her about the test results.

"I need to git it now – it's been about 6 months. I just hope I can control myself once we get together – I'm so damn horny it hurts – and to top it off I got my period too!"

"Damn girl – your shit gonna stop by Sunday?"

"It should stop by Saturday."

"Oh well – le'me go – someone's at my door – I'll call you later."

"Alright bye."

The next couple of days couldn't go by fast enough. Every night I dreamed of me and Jordan making love. Truth be told – we was out-n-out fuckin! Every position imaginable came to mind!

I got up Saturday morning and went to the bathroom. "Shit!" I yelled.

"You bang your toe again Trenice?"

"Yes Grandma."

"You need glasses Trenice? The toilet's so big — how can you miss it?"

"I guess so Grandma." I couldn't tell her I was mad as hell 'cause I still had my period and I wished it would hurry the fuck up and go away so I could get some dick tomorrow!

Chapter 15

"Woo hoo!" I yelled.

"Trenice did you hit your damn toe again?"

"No Grandma – the water's cold – I'm in the shower!"

"Oh alright."

I couldn't tell Grandma my period was gone and I could get some dick tonight. I had gone to the square earlier to pick up some candles and a nice sexy nightie.

When I got out the bathroom and went to get dressed Grandma stopped me. "Watcha got in the bag?" Before I could answer her, she grabbed my bag and pulled out my nightie. I stood there embarrassed, but I don't think Grandma noticed. "This is kinda cute but there isn't much to it."

"Oh." What else could I say? That was my grandmother!

"Your grandfather doesn't like these."

"He doesn't?"

"No – he likes for everything to be covered – then he can feel his way around."

"Grandma!"

"Well child, I'm telling you like it is!"

Chapter 16

"Hi Miss Gladys."

"Hi Jordan – where y'all goin' tonight?" Grandma knew what was up 'cause she had seen the nightie – I hoped she wasn't about to blow my shit wide open.

"Oh the usual – central park, the movies, dinner, walk around, chill."

"Well, don't have me sittin' up all night if you not comin' back tonight – let me know so I can put the chain on the door."

"Ok Grandma – we'll see ya later."

When we got downstairs Jordan asked, "Does she know?"

"Yea she knows."

"How'd she find out?"

"She went in my bag, pulled out my nightie, then proceeded to tell me what my grandfather likes."

"Grandma's open like that?"

"Yup."

We spent the majority of the morning in central park. Check in was 2p.m. so we had to find something to do until then. We figured we'd eat after we checked in. We rode the shuttle to Grand Central then took Metro North to White Plains.

"I'm glad my period's gone," I whispered in his ear.

It doesn't matter – I just want to be with you. We can just hold each other and be close – don't worry about it," he whispered back in mine.

"Well, it matters to be – I've been waitin' a long time for this and I can't wait any longer."

"To be honest, neither can I," he laughed.

When we got to White Plains it was 2 p.m. so we took a cab to the Holiday Inn Crowne Plaza. I presented my credit card and we went to the room. Once we got inside the door we looked around and we were in awe. A crystal chandelier hung from the ceiling in addition to the ceiling being mirrored. Plush peach carpeting soothed our aching feet and beige and gold furniture complimented the peach walls and carpet. There was a satin peach love seat on the left side of the room and a queen size bed on the right. A refrigerator was on the right side of the bed and the wall was mirrored behind the bed. To the left of the bed was the bathroom. The bathroom was peach, beige and gold with a Jacuzzi for two. We looked around the room then looked at each other. I went to dim the lights and pulled out the candles. I lit the candles all over the room while Jordan was in the bathroom. I took out my black and red nightie, took off my clothes, slipped on my nightie, and turned back the sheets.

"Come here Trenice."

I went into the bathroom and my eyes got wide and my mouth dropped open.

There Jordan stood, buck ass naked in the Jacuzzi. His skin was smooth all over and his body was chiseled in all the right places. His Hershey chocolate complexion glistened in the light and his ass was round and tight. When he turned to give me a full frontal view I fully understood why women were willing to drop to their knees. His cock was magnificent – smooth Hershey chocolate all over – not brown on the bottom and pink on the head like some others I had seen. His cock was hard and standing at attention – up to his belly. He stood there smiling as I stepped out of my nightie and stepped into the Jacuzzi. We turned on the shower and he soaped me up and down, taking his time in all the right places. I returned the favor, taking my time as I stroked his cock with my hands full of soap with one hand, while I grabbed his ass and pulled him close with the other. As he grabbed my ass and we explored each other's mouths with our tongues, Jordan suddenly stopped. He pushed back some and began kissing my breasts and sucking my nipples. As I leaned back my head and he continued kissing me down my body, he propped my left leg up on the Jacuzzi and began kissing, licking, and sucking on my pussy.

"Oh Jordan - don't stop," I moaned as he slid two fingers inside my pussy while he continued to kiss, lick and suck on my pussy. "Oh Jordan – I'm cumin – I'm cumin – I'm cumin…"

Jordan grabbed my ass and buried his face deep inside my pussy as I started trembling on his face…"I'm gonna eat you until you beg me to stop…"

"Don't stop – don't stop," I moaned as he continued to bury his face in my pussy and grabbed my ass again as I continued trembling on his face. He kissed, licked, and sucked on my pussy and moved his fingers in and out in unison until I gently pushed him away. He stood up, looked at me, placed the two fingers he had in my pussy in his mouth, and sucked them clean. He pulled me close to him and shoved his tongue in my mouth and I tasted my pussy on his lips and tongue for the first time. I pushed him back a little and began kissing my way down his belly until I reached his belly button, then I inserted my tongue into his belly button and licked around it. I was about to move on to his cock when he stopped me…"Something wrong?" I asked.

"Just let me look at you," he said as he tilted up my face. I closed my eyes and let the water hit my face and then he gently guided his cock to my mouth. The water beating down on his cock and the taste of it was such a turn-on for me. I kissed the left side up then licked it back down.

"Oh shit," Jordan moaned as I kissed the right side up then licked it back down. "Oh that feels so good…shit," he moaned as I licked up and down the left side then the right. I put my mouth on the tip of his cock. "Oh – oh – oh…" he moaned as I pulled my mouth away. I placed the tip of his cock in my mouth again, then the middle, then all the way down to his balls…"Oh shit," he moaned as I deep throated him. I came up some and while I still had the bulk of his cock in my mouth I swirled my tongue up and down on both sides and around without taking his cock out of my mouth…"Suck it baby – yea – that's it – suck it…oh shit…" I grabbed his ass and pushed his cock further into my mouth and sucked his cock as Jordan grabbed my head and continued to push his cock in my mouth…"Oh shit – I'm cumin…ha…ha…ha…haaaaa!!!" I swallowed every drop of his cum as he buried his cock in my mouth and his crotch in my face. When he released my head, I stood up and he pulled me close to him, kissing my lips, my nose, and my eyelids. "Torbett was a fool," he whispered in my ear.

"Did you enjoy that?"

"Hell yea..."

"Good – I just wanted to please you."

"No doubt. Did you enjoy that?"

I didn't answer right away. I tried to stop the tears but I couldn't.

"What's wrong?" Jordan asked me as he held me.

"Nothing," I said. "That was beautiful. No one has ever made me cum before – especially like that."

"You mean I was your first?"

"Yes – you were my first."

"In that case, it would be my pleasure to give you your 2nd," he said as he stepped out of the Jacuzzi, picked me up, carried me into the bedroom, and placed me on the bed.

We got under the covers and he pulled me close to him. "Your body feels so good," I said as I buried my head in his chest. I arched my back as he kissed, licked and sucked on my breasts. He continued to kiss his way down to my belly button and I spread my legs in anticipation. When I spread my legs, he stood on his knees, dropped the covers, and let me see his cock.

"Come here." I said.

He looked kinda perplexed.

"Let me rephrase that – bring him here," I said as I gently tugged on his cock."

He smiled and brought his cock to my mouth without hesitation. I put the head of his cock in my mouth, sucked a little then pushed him away. "Now," I said.

"Now what?" he cooed.

"Now I want you to fuck me," I said.

He climbed on top of me, spread my legs...

"Oh shit...Agghh!!!"

Chapter 17

When I woke up I was in a hospital bed. I lay there for a minute and tried to get my bearings. "Oh God my head hurts. What's wrong with my foot? What happened?!" I screamed as tears came to my eyes...

Jordan, Jake, Rachel, Char, Aunt Trudy, Miss April, Miss June, Grandma, and my mother all burst into the room..."Don't cry baby its ok," Grandma said as everyone stood around.

"Mom?"

"I'm here baby – it's ok."

"Where's Jordan? What happened? Why am I here?!" I screamed as more tears came down my face.

"Calm down Trenice – it's ok," Jordan said as he came into the room and hugged me.

"Well, at least I know he didn't hurt me," I thought... "Or did he?"

"Hi Trenice – I'm Dr. Campton. You had quite a night huh? We're gonna keep you here overnight for observation because you have a mild concussion."

"Concussion? Doctor what's going on? Why is my foot in a cast? Why is my head bandaged up? Will somebody please answer me?!" I screamed as I started to cry again.

"You mean they didn't tell you? Well what are you all waiting for?" Dr. Campton asked.

"Honey we think Jordan should tell you," my mother said.

I looked at Jordan and I looked at everyone else in the room. No one seemed upset with him so I said, "Can you give us some privacy?" Everyone went into the hallway but Jordan. "Jordan I'm scared – please tell me what's going on," I said as I was crying.

"Don't cry Trenice – its ok," Jordan said as he kissed my head, my eyes, my nose, and my mouth. "I'm sorry."

I had to make sure I heard right. "What did you say?"

"I'm sorry."

Now I was mad. "What the fuck did you do to me?!" I screamed.

"Calm down it wasn't my fault – I swear!"

"Then why are you sorry?"

"Let me explain."

"Okay." I figured if his family and friends and my family and friends were outside and he wasn't in jail, then he must be telling the truth.

"Ok – remember when we were in bed?"

"How could I forget?"

"Well, remember when you said you um..."

"I wanted you to fuck me?"

"Yea – that...well...the bed broke."

"Huh?"

"The frame on the bed broke, the bed hit the floor, your leg and foot got caught between the bed and the dresser, the lamp fell on your head, cut you, and you were unconscious."

"Oh my God!"

"I was so scared I didn't know what to do so I called an ambulance and the paramedics dressed you and brought you here. When they asked me who your next-next-of-kin was I told them to call your grandmother. I told her you were in an accident and she called your mother, Trudy, and Char. I called my Mum-Mums, Jake, and Rachel. I was so scared Trenice." He started to cry. "When your grandmother got here they told her how they found you and she was ready to lock my ass up for rape. The only reason she didn't have me locked up is 'cause she remember you bought that nightie."

I was quiet for a moment then I bust out laughing. I was laughing so hard I was holding my stomach.

"What the fuck are you laughing at?!" He yelled.

"This whole thing! Who the fuck's gonna believe this shit? My grandmother thought you raped me then she remembered I bought that nightie – I'm lying up in a hospital bed 'cause I wanted you to fuck me – boy oh boy did I get fucked!" We were both laughing so hard everyone came into the room.

"Everything alright Trenice?" my mother asked.

"Yes – everything's fine," I laughed.

"Visiting hours are over – everyone's gotta go," the nurse interrupted.

"Ok – hugs everyone," I said. One at a time I got my hugs and kisses from everyone.

"To be continued," Jordan whispered in my ear.

"My pleasure," I whispered back. He kissed me on the lips and left the room.

"Char? Char you still out there?"

"Yes – I'm here," she said as she came into the room.

"When I get home tomorrow I'll give you all the juicy details."

"Details? What details?"

"Let's just say I'm not an 'oral virgin' anymore."

Chapter
18

It was Tuesday afternoon. Shit! There goes that nosy fuckin' bitch...Oh God – here she comes...

"You alright Trenice?"

"Yes Sissy – I'm ok."

"I heard what happened ‑ damn girl he really laid you out huh?" Everyone around was laughing. Jordan cut his eyes at her like he wanted to knock the shit out of her.

"Excuse me ‑ I need to get her in the house."

Sissy cut her eyes back at Jordan but she moved out the way so Jordan could wheel me into the building.

"Damn Trenice – you alright?" Tony asked.

"She's Fine!" Jordan growled. He bounced the wheel chair up the stairs and Tony went out the door without saying a word.

"Hi Miss Gladys."

"Hi Jordan – come on in – wait a minute – let me move the couch," she said as she pulled the couch away from the wall some. My mother and Aunt Trudy were there too.

"Honey help me up outta this wheelchair."

"You don't need to be on that foot Trenice," my grandmother said.

"I know Grandma but I can hop – and I gotta pee." They all hollered as I hopped down the hall.

I had to push myself on the back of the toilet and extend my leg so I could pee. I hit my broke foot on the tub…"Aagghh!!" I couldn't stop the stampede from comin' down the hall…the door burst open and there they stood: Grandma, my mother, Jordan, and Aunt Trudy. My pants were down around my ankles.

"Sorry – we just wanted to make sure you were ok," my mother said.

"Jordan can you help me please?"

"That's how you got in this mess in the first place Trenice – hasn't he help you enough?" My mother and Aunt Trudy laughed along with my grandmother.

"Oh I'm never gonna live this down am I Trenice?" Jordan asked.

"You? I live here – what about me?"

Jordan pulled my panties up to my waist, stood me up, pulled up my pants, and I leaned on him as I hobbled down the hall.

"I gotta get going – I'll come check on ya later. "By Miss Gladys – bye Trudy – bye Miss...Trenice what's your Mother's name?"

"Claire."

"Bye Miss Claire." He kissed me then went out the door.

"Alright Ma – we gonna go too," my mother said.

"Alright Claire, Trudy – see ya tomorrow."

"Trenice you call me if you need anything."

"I will Ma."

When they closed the door behind them I tried to hop into the kitchen but I tripped and hit the wall.

"Dammit Trenice - will you sit your ass down before you break your other damn foot!" my grandmother yelled.

"Ok Grandma – I'm sitting." I sat down for a minute and got back up – this time I put the pressure on my left foot and I used the rubber heel on my right foot.

"Trenice are you in the fridge?"

"Yes Grandma."

"Bring me a soda."

Chapter 19

On Wednesday I went to see Char. It had been a week and ½ since I left the hospital and I was hobbling around pretty well. Char sat there with her mouth open and her eyes wide while I gave her all the details.

"Whoa! I guess we know the answer to the 'eat pussy' question huh?" she said as we bust out laughing. "Well girl you know that man I been seeing?"

"Yea Char I remember." I said. I loved Char but I hated that she only dated married men. Just last week she was telling me that she was tired of seeing married men and she wanted her own man. "I thought you were breaking it off with him?"

"I was girl, but we did it again."

"You did?"

"Girl he is so smooth. I told him to put my legs up on his shoulders so I could feel all of him but he was so big I told him oh I can't take all of you – put my legs back down," she laughed.

"Char I don't want you to get hurt – what if his wife finds out?"

"Oh she won't but don't worry – I'm not tryin' to wind up dead – I don't go to his house or his job – he comes here."

"Well be careful girl."

"I will Trenice. I wish he'd leave his wife. He told me he wants to but he can't 'cause it will cost him too much and he'll lose everything."

"Char don't let him get away with that. He could string you along for years. You deserve better."

"Oh so now you know what's best for me 'cause you finally got a man? That makes you an expert? Who the fuck do you think you are?"

"Bye Char," I said as I got up from the kitchen table and went out the front door.

"Bye!" she yelled as I closed it. Sigh.

Chapter 20

It had been 3 weeks since I left the hospital. Jordan came by every night to see me and make sure I was ok. Sissy hasn't said another word to me since that day outside.

"Jordan what'd you say to Sissy?" Aunt Trudy asked.

"I didn't say shit to her!" This was only the 2nd time I had heard Jordan raise his voice.

"I just asked – don't bite my head off!"

"And I just told you."

"Le'me go Ma – see you later," she said as she slammed the door behind her.

"Bye Trudy," Jordan said as he kissed me hello. "How are you sweet heart?" he asked.

"I'm ok now that you're here but there's something I gotta do."

"What's that?" he asked as he watched me pick up the phone...

"Tyler Marshall Law Offices may I help you?"

"Yes – I'd like to make an appointment."

"How's next Monday at 10 a.m.?"

"Monday's fine."

"Your name?"

"Trenice Robertson."

"Can you give me a few details?"

"I'm filing suit against the Holiday Inn Crowne Plaza."

"Can you be more specific?"

"Not at this time."

"Ok Ms. Robertson I'll see you next Monday."

"Thank you."

"Are you serious?" Jordan asked.

"Damn right – I could'a broke my back."

"I hear you. Oh – before I forget – Jake and Rachel want us to hang out with them this weekend – you up for that?"

"I'm not sure I can be on my foot that long honey."

"We won't go far."

"Okay – long as we don't go too far." I didn't see Jordan again until the weekend.

Chapter 21

Jordan came to pick me up – literally. "I'm goin' now Grandma."

"Alright – be careful."

"Ok I will Grandma."

"Bye Miss Gladys," Jordan said.

"Jordan?"

"Yes Miss Gladys?"

"Stay away from the Holiday Inn," she laughed.

We just looked at each other, then he picked me up and he carried me down the stairs. "Two more weeks," he whispered in my ear as he helped me in the car.

"My pleasure," I whispered back.

"How you doin' Trenice – how's your foot?" Jake asked.

"I'm ok but I'd be better if people would stop with the jokes. My grandmother just HAD TO tell us to stay away from the Holiday Inn," I said as we all bust out laughing.

"Shit we been fuckin' for years and we never broke the damn bed," Rachel said as we all laughed again.

"Well, we didn't even get a chance to fuck and the damn bed broke," I said as we all laughed again.

"Imagine what'll happen when we finally do fuck," Jordan said. It was quite for a minute or so.

"Don't use the bed," Jake laughed.

"Ya know – that's not a bad idea," I laughed. We all laughed again. "That's why I'm suing their ass."

"You are?" Jake and Rachel asked.

"Hell yea – I could'a broke my back!"

"I hear that – they tried to break your back now break that bank," Rachel said as we all laughed again.

"I got me a good ‑ass lawyer too – Tyler Marshall & Associates. They specialize in personal injury and I didn't have to give them a retainer."

"I hear you girl," Rachel said.

We went to Tads for dinner, as usual, and laughed and talked for hours. The waiter didn't mind 'cause we kept eatin' and gettin' refills on iced tea so he knew he would be gettin' a nice tip. After dessert, we all got up to go back to the car. We drove to central park and sat there until the stars came out. Then, we all got in the car and Jake drove us home. When we got to Yonkers I asked, "Jake can you drop Jordan and I off at the park?"

"Sure."

"Trenice I gotta get up for work tomorrow – can it wait?" Jordan asked.

"I guess," I sighed.

"C'mon we'll go to the park."

"Ok – thanks Jake," I said.

"You're welcome Trenice – good night."

"Good night."

When we were alone in the park Jordan asked, "What's this about Trenice?"

"I wanted to ask ya something."

"Ok – what?"

"How do you feel about anal sex?"

Jordan just sat their quiet.

"Jordan did you hear me?"

"I heard you."

"Well?"

"That's some freaky shit."

"Yea it is."

"Let me get you home so I can get up for work tomorrow."

"Ok – let's go."

We smiled at each other as he picked me up, carried me down the stairs, and put me in the cab. When we got home he carried me upstairs and Sissy was in the hallway.

"Hi Sissy," I sneered. Sissy went into her apartment and slammed the door as Jordan put me down. "Two weeks," he whispered in my ear.

"My pleasure," I whispered back as we kissed each other goodnight.

Grandma was in the kitchen making herself a cup of coffee when I came in. "You gonna get that cast off soon huh Trenice?"

"Yep."

"You gonna stay away from that damn Holiday Inn?" she laughed.

"Good night Grandma," I said as I ignored her question.

"Good night Trenice," she said as she went down the hall to her bedroom.

I went into the kitchen, got a pen and some paper out the kitchen drawer, and sat at the table to write a song by candlelight:

<u>Sexy Chocolate</u>

VS I   Never felt this way before and I'm not ashamed. Everyone around can see you're the one to blame. Wrap your arms around me darlin' – I'm in ecstasy. Tonight I want us to create the perfect fantasy.

Change   I'm gonna take you and I hope that you're prepared, 'Cause where we're goin' can never be compared. I want you and I know that you want me. When we get together, we'll make history because you're....

Chorus I   Sweeter than a sugar plum
(sexy chocolate),
and I'm gonna get me some
(sexy chocolate).
Sweeter than a lollipop (sexy chocolate),
tasty down to the last drop
(sexy chocolate).

VS II   Looking forward to the time we can
           be alone. Hurry, come to me my
           love, disconnect the phone. Hunger
           for your touch my darlin' - I'm filled
           with desire! You ignite this passion,
           now come put out the fire!

Repeat Change

Repeat Chorus I

VS III   Pull me closer to your body, wanna
           taste your lips. Lay me down and
           work it baby, grab hold of my hips.
           Slide yourself between my thighs
           right where I want it. Give me
           every inch of your sexy chocolate.

Repeat Change

Repeat Chorus I

Chorus II   Sweet (sexy chocolate).
            Feels so good to me baby.
            (sexy chocolate).
            Tasty, and sexy (sexy chocolate).
            And sweet (sexy chocolate).

Chapter 22

I got to the lawyer's office at 9:30 a.m. The receptionist greeted me. "Ms.Robertson you're early. Would you like some coffee while you wait?"

"Yes please."

"You sure you don't wanna tell me what this is about?"

"You'll find out soon enough," I said with a laugh.

"It must be a doozy."

"You don't know the half of it," I said as I sat down and drank my coffee. Just as I was finishing my coffee Tyler came out into the lobby.

"Ms.Robertson I'm Mr. Marshall – please come into my office."

"Please call me Trenice," I said as I went into his office and closed the door.

"Very well, you can call me Tyler. Now what's this - I see you want to sue the Holiday Inn Crowne Plaza for $1,000,000?? What the hell did they do to you?"

Everyone in the office was standing outside the door when I opened it an hour later. Tyler couldn't control his laughter and neither could I. We looked around the office, looked at each other, and laughed some more.

"Ms. Robertson please tell me what's going on – you seem mighty happy for someone filling a million dollar law suit!" the receptionist said.

"Tyler will fill you all in I'm sure," I laughed.

"Trenice make sure your boyfriend comes to see me ASAP!"

"I will Tyler – and thank you for taking the case."

"Oh I wouldn't miss this for the world!" he said as I left the building.

The cab was waiting for me when I got downstairs. I got my first disability check for $250 but that would be gone in a minute by the time I paid for cabs back and forth to the law office in White Plains, the hospital, and back to Yonkers. After I left the hospital, I had the cab take me to Getty Square and wait.

"I charge extra for waiting miss."

"You'll get your money don't worry."

"You give me $40 now or I leave." He was charging me $40 for the trip from the law office, then to the hospital, the wait at the hospital, then the trip to Yonkers. "Ok here," I said as I handed him a $100 bill.

"Ok you go and I wait," he said.

"Ok you give me my $60 change then I go," I said. This motherfucker wasn't running out on me with my $100 – I ain't that fuckin' stupid!

"Here," he said as he threw three $20 bills at me.

"Never mind, you can go now – I'll get another cab," I said as I picked up the $20 bills, got out the cab, and slammed the fuckin' door. That jackass blew a $20 tip. Oh well, his loss.

I went through the store and smiled when I saw Jordan.

"What are you doing here?" he asked.

"You go to lunch yet?"

"No why?"

"Let's go – I got a lot to tell ya."

"Ok – yo John – I'm out – I'll be back at 2," he yelled.

"Alright Jordan – see ya later."

As we went through the store, one of Jordan's associates held the door for us so we could walk out. Jordan went to get the cab and I waited in the foyer. His associate approached me.

"Trenice can I ask you something?"

"Sure."

"What's he got that I haven't got?"

"Me," I said as Jordan came back to escort me to the cab.

"What was that about?"

"You," I said as I got in the cab. Jordan smiled as he went around and got in on the other side. We went to the Parkside Dinner for lunch. While we were waiting for our order I gave Jordan the 411.

"Are you serious?"

"Hell yea I'm serious."

"But I didn't get hurt."

"The hell you didn't."

"What do you mean?"

"When I got hurt in that hotel, you were scared to death. You were emotionally traumatized. You were only trying to make love to me and you wound up in the hospital being accused of rape. Imagine if my grandmother didn't remember I bought that nightie? You would've spent the night in jail for nothing – and even though I wouldn't have pressed charges, everyone would look at you as a rapist."

"But it didn't happen."

"That's not the point. It could have."

"I just don't think it's a good idea."

"Ok – try this on for size – what about alienation of affection?"

"What the hell is that?"

"You and I had every intention of making love. Since the incident at the hotel we haven't been able to finish consummating our relationship due to their negligence."

Jordan sat there with his mouth wide open. He stared at me in disbelief. "You're right. I never thought about it that way. And I was scared."

"Exactly."

"I'll contact Tyler Marshall right away."

"Good."

We finished lunch and Jordan helped me to the cab he had waiting outside for us. The cab dropped him off at work and before he got out the cab, I took the song out of my pocket and gave it to him. He kissed me good bye and I had the cab drop me off at Char's house.

Chapter 23

It had been almost 3 weeks since I'd seen Char. Char wasn't home so I waited outside for about 30 minutes. I missed my best friend. I wanted to apologize to her for upsetting her and I wanted my best friend back. I wanted to share my good news. My happiness was short-lived when she drove up with the married man.

"Watchu doin' here?!"

"I miss my friend."

"I miss my friend too," she said as she helped me up and we hugged.

"I'm sorry," we said to each other with tears in our eyes. We went upstairs and sat in the kitchen.

"I was mad at you because you were right Trenice."

"I just want you to have someone who loves you and only you. You're so special and you shouldn't have to hide and sneak around."

"We don't sneak around anymore girl," she said with a smile.

"Oh my God what happened? Details girl – details!"

"Well I thought about what you said and I told him I was tired of sneaking around - I wanted to be out in the open and have a real relationship."

"What'd he say?"

"He showed me separation papers girl!"

"Stop it! Really?"

"Yup. He got a legal separation from his wife. The divorce will be final in about 6 months. You know that bitch ain't letting go without a fight."

"I'm so happy for you Char. Looks like we both hit the jackpot."

"Girl, Jordan is the best thing that's happened to you in a long time."

"Yes he is – oh I forgot to tell you what's goin' on now…"

"What Trenice? Ya'll gettin' married?"

"I wish – but let me tell ya."

"Ok – what?"

"We're suing the Holiday Inn Crowne Plaza for $1,000,000!"

"Girl, you ain't gonna git that money."

"Oh we'll get some money alright. They'll be happy to settle when I get through with them."

"I hate to burst your bubble Trenice, but you ain't gettin' no real money. They'll probably just give you a couple thousand and pay your medical bills."

"Not when Tyler Marshall & Associates gets through with their ass."

"Tyler Marshall? How the fuck can you afford him?"

"That's the best part – personal injury doesn't require a retainer – they get paid when you get paid."

"Girl you go – let me know what happens."

"You haven't heard the best part."

"What's that?"

"Jordan and I are also filing a suit for alienation of affection."

"What's that?"

"Well, since the incident, we haven't been able to fuck. It was their negligence that caused it." She laughed out loud.

"Where the fuck did you get that idea?"

"When I went for my workman's comp/disability hearing this woman was filing suit against her company 'cause the floor was wet. They didn't put up a sign and she fell and hurt her back. Her husband was filing a suit for alienation of affection. His lawyer said that because of their negligence, his wife couldn't perform her marital duties."

"Then damn – you about to get paid 'cause you can't get no dick!" she laughed.

"Yea – I can't get fucked so I'm fuckin' them!" We hollered at that one.

Chapter 24

When I got home I told Grandma about the law suit (I didn't tell her about the alienation of affection part though).

"Good – you should sue their ass – I don't know how much money you gonna get though."

"What money?" I turned around and there was Aunt Trudy and her nosy bitch ass friend Sissy. Just what the fuck I needed.

"I'm suing the hotel."

"Good – sue 'em then we can get paid."

"We?"

"Yea – I know you gonna share with family."

"No the fuck I'm not either," I thought to myself. I knew better than to say that shit out loud. Jordan knocked on the door just in time.

"Hi Jordan," Aunt Trudy said as he kissed me hello.

"Hello Trudy, Sissy, Miss Gladys."

"Hi Jordan," Grandma said. "Sissy don't be rude – say hello."

"That's ok Miss Gladys – you ready Trenice?"

"Yes," I said as I stood up and headed for the door.

"We'll see ya later," Jordan said.

"By Grandma, Aunt Trudy, Sissy." I was so glad to get the fuck outta there. When we got in the cab I said, "I'm tellin' Grandma about the suit and here comes Aunt Trudy with that nosy bitch talking about we gettin' paid!"

"What?"

"Yea – she talkin' 'bout she know I'm gonna share with family – yea right – in her fuckin' dreams!" We both laughed as we headed to Jordan's house.

Chapter 25

When we got to Jordan's house, Miss April and Miss June started right in.

"Hi Trenice – how's your foot?"

"This cast comes off in two weeks."

"They sure don't make beds like they used to huh?" Miss April said.

"They sure don't," Miss June said as they both bust out laughing. Jordan and I just shook our heads.

"Jordan I wanna stop and see my mother ok?"

"You want me to go with you?"

"Sure," I said. We went out in the hall and all you heard was 'thump, thump, thump' as my rubber heel hit the steps.

"Mommy – Trenice is here!" my little sister yelled as she opened the door. Jordan came in behind me.

"Are you the man that broke my sister's foot? Why did you do that?" My mother, brothers, and sisters all bust out laughing.

"It's not funny – he hurt my sister!" she cried.

"It's ok Bunny," I said as I hugged her.

"I'm sorry Bunny," Jordan said. "I didn't mean to hurt Trenice. I love her and I'll never hurt her again. Do you forgive me?"

"That's the same shit my Daddy said to me every time he hit my Mommy!" she screamed and ran into the room crying. Everyone got quiet. Jordan looked at me then at my mother. I got up to go in the room.

"Leave her alone Trenice," my mother said.

"No – I'm gonna talk to my sister."

"Trenice – you're mother's right," Jordan tried to explain but I cut him off...

"No she isn't right! Don't you see what just happened? We're all old enough to deal with this but she doesn't understand – all she knows is you're gonna do to me what my father did to my mother!" I had never yelled at Jordan like that before. We didn't see Bunny standing there...

"Stop it! Leave my Mommy alone!" she screamed."

"I'm sorry Bunny – I'm sorry," I cried as I hugged her.

"Don't cry Trenice, don't cry," she said.

"Maybe we better go Trenice," Jordan said.

"Maybe you're right," I said as I got we got up to leave.

"Sit down Trenice," my mother said. We sat down.

"You don't have to go anywhere. I wish I didn't put you all through that shit," she said with tears in her eyes.

"Mom it wasn't your fault...let's talk about something else."

"Ok," she said as she wiped her eyes. I told her all about the law suit as she made us coffee. My brothers and sisters just sat and listened.

"Good – I could use a new car," she said. Jordan and I looked at each other and shook our heads. I got up from the table.

"Where you goin' Trenice?" my mother asked.

"I'm going to talk to Bunny Mom."

"Trenice don't upset her any more. She's been through enough."

"I know Mom but you need to get her some help."

"Don't tell me how to raise my child Trenice."

"I'm not Mom, but there's a play group in White Plains called the Stepping Stone. The children play and as they act out their aggressions, the social workers help them deal with their issues."

"What the hell do you know about a group like that?"

"They helped me a lot," I said as I went into the room to talk to Bunny.

"Hi Bunny. Can we talk?"

"Uh huh."

"Jordan didn't mean to hurt me Bunny. It was an accident."

"But Daddy always said that to Mommy Trenice."

"But Daddy hit Mommy – Jordan didn't hit me Bunny."

"He didn't?" she perked.

"No Bunny. We sat on the bed to go to sleep and the bed broke." I sat on her bed to show her what happened and I placed my foot between the bed and dresser to show her how it happened.

"See Bunny?"

"Yea....Trenice?"

"Yes?"

"If you wanted to go to sleep, why didn't you just go back to Grandma's house? Then you wouldn't have broken your foot." I laughed to myself as she ran into the kitchen.

"Jordan lets go downstairs now ok?"

"Ok Trenice – By Miss Claire – nice to meet you all," he said.

"Bye Jordan," Bunny said as she gave him a hug.

"Bye Bunny," he said as he hugged her back and smiled. We left to go downstairs.

When we got out in the hallway Jordan said, "You wanna talk about what just happened?"

"No," I said. He pulled me close to him and held me for a few minutes.

"I'm sorry I yelled at you like that."

"It's ok – don't worry about it – what did you say to Bunny to make her so happy?"

"I told her the truth."

"You did? You told her everything?"

"She's only 9 Jordan."

"Oh – right. But what did you tell her?"

"I told her we sat on the bed to go to sleep and the bed broke."

"What did she say?"

"She said I should'a went home – then I wouldn't have broken my foot."

"Oh I see." We bust out laughing as I 'thumped' downstairs while Jordan followed.

When we got inside Miss April's house, Jordan took the song from his metal box.

"I like this…"

"Me too…"

"So you want every inch of me huh?" he said as he pulled me close to him and began kissing my neck.

"Every inch," I whispered as we began exploring each other's mouth with our tongues.

"Ahem!" Miss April and Miss June interrupted.

"Excuse us," we said in unison. We all laughed as Jordan walked me downstairs and put me in the cab.

Chapter 26

"Jordan go see that lawyer yet?"

"He's goin' today Grandma."

"Good – the sooner the better – and don't pay your Aunt Trudy no mind – you know she always lookin' to get something for nothin'."

"I know Grandma." Little did she know I had already taken that advice about a few people..."Grandma?"

"Yea Trenice?"

"What do you want me to buy you when I get paid?"

"Trenice you don't owe me anything."

"I know Grandma but can I buy you something? You've always been there for me and so many other people – you deserve something nice."

"Thank you baby but I don't want anything," she said as she kissed my forehead. Grandma should've known I wasn't payin' her any mind.

"Who is it?" she called out as she went to answer the door.

"Jordan." I hobbled to the door.

"You keep hobbling like that Trenice you gonna break that other foot," she said as she let Jordan in.

"Hi Miss Gladys," he said as he sat down.

"How'd everything go?" Grandma asked.

"It went ok. He said we should hear from them by next week. You ready Trenice?"

"Yup."

"Bye Miss Gadys."

"Bye Grandma."

"See ya later," Grandma called out from the bedroom.

After we got in the cab Jordan said, "Since I didn't have to work today, why don't we stop by Jake and Rachel's?"

"Ok." When we got there they were waiting outside. "They knew we were comin' didn't they?"

"Yea – I called them earlier. You mind?"

"No – we gonna stay here?"

"Nope."

"Where we goin'?"

"You'll see." A limo pulled up and Jake and Rachel got in the car. "C'mon Trenice," he said as he opened the door for me. I got in the car with them and we drove off. So far everything looked the same until we got to New York City. I noticed we were on the west side and we turned at 59th Street.

"Why are we going this way honey?"

"You'll see." We kept going until we stopped in front of the Mark Helinger Theatre.

"Surprise!" they all yelled.

"Thanks but what's the occasion?" Jordan pulled two tickets out of his jacket and handed them to me.

"Oh my God – Smokey Robinson?"

"Yes – Smokey Robinson." He helped me out the car and we went inside.

I fell asleep on the way home from the concert. When I woke up we were almost home. "Smokey Robinson gets better and better – I wish tonight didn't have to end," I said as we pulled up in front of Grandma's house."

"Maybe it doesn't have to end," Jordan whispered in my ear. We had dropped off Jake and Rachel so it was just the two of us.

"I'm so tempted," I whispered as we kissed each other.

"Then what's stopping you?" he whispered as he kissed my neck...

"You two gettin' out here or can I take you somewhere?" For a minute I'd forgotten the limo driver was in the limo with us.

"I'll get out here," I said before Jordan could answer.

"Less than two weeks," he whispered in my ear."

"My pleasure," I whispered back. He helped me out the limo and, as luck would have it, my Aunt Trudy's nosy bitch as friend, Sissy was right on time...

"Where you goin' all dressed up?"

"To bed," I said. I kept going until I got upstairs without looking back.

Chapter 27

It was Friday and I hadn't seen Jordan since Tuesday night. I missed him so much and I was tired of staying in the house.

"One more week and this stupid cast comes off – then I can get my life back – and I can get some dick too," I thought to myself.

The phone rang and I snatched it up hoping it was Jordan. "Hello," I said cheerfully.

"Trenice its Tyler. I have some bad news."

"What's wrong?"

"Well, I don't know how to put this...but they laughed at your suit."

"They laughed?"

"I'm sorry Trenice. They offered to pay your medical bills and give you $20,000. That's it."

"Tyler?"

"Yes Trenice?"

"Can you set up a meeting with their lawyers?"

"Trenice they've made up their mind."

"I hear ya, but I've got an idea."

"What's that?"

"Well, I may not get $1,000,000 but they might be willing to settle if I threatened to go to the press."

"Trenice, that won't get you any money."

"I know it won't but by the time I get through telling my story to ABC, NBC, CBS, and CNN, how many people are gonna be willing to get a room for a night of romance at the Holiday Inn Crowne Plaza if they're afraid the bed will break? I don't think the Holiday Inn Crowne Plaza will like that kind of publicity."

"I like your idea Trenice. You may not get any money but this will ruin their reputation. Who knows — you could even get a book outta this," he laughed.

"I'll call you later this afternoon."

"Thanks Tyler."

"You're welcome Trenice."

"Hello," I said as I picked up the phone again.

"You don't sound too happy to hear from me."

"Jordan!"

"Now that's more like it! Now what's wrong?"

"Tyler just called."

"Well?"

"They offered to pay my medical bills and give me $20,000."

"Take it Trenice – it's better than nothing."

"I asked Tyler to set up a meeting with their lawyers. He's gonna call me back."

"Trenice you sure you wanna go ahead with this? Maybe you should take the money and run."

"Tyler thinks it's a good idea. He says I may not get any money but it could ruin their reputation."

"Why do it if you don't think you can get any money?"

"Jordan I know we won't get a million dollars but we could get more than $20,000."

"We could also get nothing."

"If I settle for $20,000, after the law firm takes 33% plus their fees, it will be as if I settled for nothing."

"See what Tyler says when he calls you back – then we'll see."

"Ok Jordan."

"I gotta run..."

"Jordan?"

"Yes?"

"I love you."

"I love you too Trenice."

"See you tonight?"

"See you tonight."

I sat there staring at the phone all misty eyed.

"Whatsa matter with you?" Grandma asked as she came down the hall.

"Oh nothing," I sighed.

"I'll be glad when you get that damn cast off – you need to get outside and get some air...

"Hello?" I snatched the phone up on the first ring.

"Trenice?"

"Yes Tyler?"

"They'll meet with us tomorrow morning."

"Wow that was quick."

"Don't get your hopes up Trenice. I like your idea but as your lawyer I must advise you that this may not work."

"I know Tyler. I appreciate everything you've done for me and your willingness to even take the case no matter what happens.

"Well I'm glad you appreciate me Trenice, but appreciation don't pay the rent," he laughed.

"I hear ya. What time tomorrow?"

"10 a.m."

"Ok – see ya then."

"Who you on the phone with now?" Grandma asked as I called Jordan.

"I'm callin' Jordan Grandma."

"You need to let the man work Trenice."

"I know Grandma but this is important..."

"Aren't you gonna see him tonight?"

"Yea but..."   I was totally unaware that Jordan had answered and heard this exchange...

"Helllooooo?"

"Oh sorry Jordan – Tyler called. We have an appointment tomorrow at 10 a.m."

"On Saturday?"

"That's what I said too."

"Ok – I'll see ya later then."

"Ok."   After I hung up the phone I told Grandma about the meeting.

"You should've taken the $20,000 Trenice. Now you probably won't get anything," she said as she went down the hall.

Chapter 28

Jordan came to pick me up after work.

"I'm glad you're here Jordan — if it weren't for you Trenice wouldn't go outside at all!"

"I know Miss Gladys. We'll see ya later."

I started to tell Grandma I didn't go outside 'cause I didn't feel like sitting outside with Aunt Trudy and nosy ass Sissy but I just kept quiet and left with Jordan.

When we got to Jordan's house I asked, "Jordan, can we go see my mother?"

"You sure?"

"Yea."

"Oooookkkaaayyy...," he said as I 'thumped' upstairs. When we got to the top of the stairs Jordan pulled me close to him and began nibbling on my neck.

"One more week," he whispered as he kissed my neck and caressed my nipples through my blouse.

"My pleasure," I moaned as I rubbed his cock through his pants. He pulled my face to his and kissed me with so much passion my clit was stinging.

"Oooohhhh... Mommy, Trenice and Jordan are kissing!" Bunny yelled as she came up the stairs. We jumped when we heard her.

"Bunny!" I breathed, "You scared me!"

"Tee hee hee...," she said as she knocked on the door.

"Hello Jordan, Hello Trenice, come on in," my mother said.

"Hello Miss Claire."

"Mommy I saw Jordan and Trenice kissing," Bunny said.

"Uh huh, that's how you wound up with that cast on your foot," my mother laughed.

"No it isn't Mommy," Bunny said. We all turned around to look at her. I was praying my mother wouldn't correct her and go into a lengthy explanation – sometimes parents give their children too much information too soon, or too little information too late. I remember when my brothers were 9 and 10 and she'd tell them, "When you get older, don't listen to what the girl says – use a condom." When they'd ask, "Why?"

she'd say, "You'll find out when you get older." What was the point in mentioning it if she wasn't going to explain it? Anyway, thank God she didn't try to correct Bunny.

"Mommy – I had so much fun today – and guess what Mommy? My friend Suzie goes there too!"

"That's good honey."

"Mom, where'd she go?" I asked as Bunny went to change her clothes.

"The Stepping Stone," she said. Jordan and I looked at each other and smiled.

"So what brings you here?" my mother asked.

"I spoke to Tyler today."

"What'd he say?" "

"Well Mom, they only offered to pay my medical bills and give me $20,000. We have a meeting tomorrow morning with their lawyers at 10 a.m."

"Trenice maybe you should've accepted their offer."

"We'll see what happens tomorrow Mom."

"Don't get your hopes up Trenice."

"I won't Mom don't worry. Besides, how can I buy you a car with $5,000?"

"$5,000? What happened to $20,000?"

"33% plus fees goes to my lawyer," I said.

"You mean 65%," my mother said as we all laughed.

"Mom, it's gettin' late and I wanna go see Miss April and Miss June before I go."

"Alright – tell them I said hello."

"I will Mom – good night."

"Good night."

"Good night Miss Claire," Jordan said.

"Bye Trenice, bye Jordan!" Bunny yelled.

"Bye Bunny!" we yelled back.

Miss April heard me 'thumpin' downstairs and opened the door. "You can't sneak up on nobody can ya?" she laughed.

"Hi Miss April" I said as we went into the house.

"Hi Mum-Mum," Jordan said. I laughed when Miss April told me how when Jordan was little they tried to teach him to say Grandma and Mamma but all he could say was Mum-Mum - and he's been calling them both Mum-Mum ever since.

We told Miss April and Miss June about my conversations with Tyler.

"I'm glad you didn't accept the $20,000 – you'll probably get more," Miss April said. I couldn't believe my ears.

"Huh? You're the first person to tell me that Miss April – even Jordan said I should've taken the $20,000."

"Trenice was smart not to take that money," Miss June said.

"Why Mum?"

"Because you never take the first offer. I worked for the County Attorney's office for 20 years. If they offer you $20,000 they can go as high as $50,000."

"Wow!" I screamed.

"Calm down Trenice – I don't want you to get your hopes up. I'm just sayin' that if they offered you twenty, thay can go a little higher." Visions of dollar signs danced in my head...

"Trenice, I better get you home – we have an interesting day tomorrow."

"Ok – good night Miss April, good night Miss June."

"See ya in a bit Mum-Mum."

When we got to Grandma's house, Aunt Trudy and nosy ass Sissy were sitting outside.

"You hear from that lawyer yet?" Sissy yelled to the whole building.

"Not yet," I lied. Jordan and I hurried into the building and up the stairs so we wouldn't have to carry on a conversation. Soon as we got in the house here comes Aunt Trudy right behind us.

"Hey Jordan."

"Hey Trudy."

"Trenice you ain't hear from that lawyer yet?"

"No," I lied.

"Trenice I thought you said you had an appointment tomorrow at 10 a.m.," Grandma yelled.

Shit! – I was almost caught – then I had an idea: "No Grandma – I called and they said he was in court and he wouldn't be available until after 10 a.m. tomorrow."

"Oohh."

"Ma, come outside – me and Sissy sittin' downstairs," Aunt Trudy said.

"Ok – soon as I get out the bathroom," Grandma said.

When Grandma went outside I said, "Jordan you better go before my Grandma comes back with Aunt Trudy, Sissy, and more questions," I laughed.

"You're right – good night."

"Good night – I love you."

"I love you too." I got in bed and pretended to be asleep when Grandma, Sissy, and Aunt Trudy came in the house, gossiping about the commotion outside.

Chapter 29

Jordan came to pick me up for an early breakfast Saturday morning. It was perfect – I got out of the house while everyone was still asleep. Even the neighbors sleep late on Saturday, so we were good to go...or so I thought...

"What chall doin' up so early?"

"Hi Sissy," I said. "Shit – where the fuck did she come from?" I thought to myself...then I saw the laundry cart..."I see you doin' laundry."

"Yea girl – gotta git them machines before 12:00 – where y'all off too?"

"Breakfast."

"Alright – see ya later."

"Ok Sissy," I said as we got in the cab.

"Whew – that was a close one huh?"

"50 Main Street, White Plains," Jordan told the driver. "Let's just do this – then we can eat."

"Sounds good to me," I said.

We got to Tyler's office at 10 a.m. sharp. "C'mon Trenice – let's hurry up," Jordan said.

"They can wait a minute," I said.

"Good morning Trenice, Jordan – this is Bernice Thomas and Gordan Smith," Tyler said as he introduced us. "They represent the Holiday Inn Crowne Plaza."

"Good morning, good morning," we said as we all shook hands and sat down. Tyler's secretary came into the room.

"Coffee anyone?"

"Yes please," I said. She brought in a coffee pot, cups, creamer, sugar, and spoons then she cracked the door. I could see her listening but I didn't mind. I just hoped she didn't get caught. The court reporter prepared her machine and we began.

After the 'state your name and address for the record, etc.' Bernice spoke. "Miss Robertson, Mr. Williams we've gone over your papers and I'm sorry but our offer stands. Take it or leave it." Now the fun was to begin.

"Your offer stands? I wish your mattress stood like your offer – then maybe we wouldn't be spending Saturday morning in this fuckin' office..."

Bernice's eyes damn nearly popped out of her head along with Tyler's and Jordan's.

"Miss Robertson, please," Gordon interjected.

"Please what? Huh?"

I got so close to that man Jordan and Tyler stood up at the same time. Jordan put his hand on my shoulder and Tyler sat back down. I remained standing, but I was nowhere through...

"Please what?!" I got even louder. "Please forget that I could've broken my back? Please forget that the hotel staff and paramedics saw me sprawled out ass out? Please forget that what was supposed to be a night of passion turned into the night from hell? Please forget that I got a permanent fuckin' scar on my forehead? Please forget that Jordan was accused of raping me? Is that what you want me to do? Huh? You want me to pretend I don't have the fuckin' cast on my foot? Huh?"

Bernice and Gordon began to back away from me as I continued ranting and raving at the top of my lungs...

"You want me to forget about that fuckin' concussion I got? Huh? You want me to forget all the ridiculing I've had to put up with? Huh? All the fuckin' bed jokes? You want me to forget about my lost wages? Oh I got disability – fuckin' $250 for one month but I should be glad right?

Well fuck that and fuck both of you 'cause that's about all I've been able to do for the past 5 weeks!"

Tyler and Jordan were stunned. I could hear Tyler's secretary laughing outside the door. No one said anything – they just sat there while the court reporter got it all down, so I started up again.

"Ya know, it would've been nice if you pretended to give a damn – maybe even offer a fake ass apology, but no – that would have been too humane!"

"Maybe this wasn't such a good idea," Bernice said.

"Oh it was a great idea," I said.

They all looked perplexed.

"I bet ABC, NBC, CBS, and CNN will think it's a great idea too. How many people do you think will wanna stay at the Holiday Inn Crowne Plaza after they get a hold of this story?"

"Perhaps we were a little insensitive Miss Robertson. We do, at the very least, owe you an apology," Bernice said.

"Yes – it appears you have suffered a great deal," Gordon said.

"It appears? What – you need fuckin' glasses?!" I was up on my feet so fast Tyler and Jordan got up and Jordan stepped in front of me... "Miss Thomas was right – this was a complete waist of time – let's go Jordan," I said as I got up to get my coat...

"Miss Robertson – wait...," Bernice said. "Perhaps we could make you another offer..."

I sat back down while Bernice and Gordon whispered to each other. Then Bernice leaned over and whispered something to Tyler. Tyler wrote something on a piece of paper and handed it to me. I looked at the paper and smiled. Jordan looked at me then at the paper. He smiled as he read the following amounts: $500,000, $100,000. He handed me back the paper and I handed it back to Tyler. I nodded in agreement but didn't smile. Jordan was looking at me as if to say, "What's wrong?"

"My clients have agreed to your offer," Tyler said as he winked at me.

"Very good. We'll have the papers in your office next week," Bernice said as she and Gordon stood up. They walked out without saying good bye. Jordan looked at me.

"Aren't you happy?"

"They gone yet?" I asked.

"Yes, they're gone," Tyler said.

"Woooo hooo!" I yelled and we all gave each other high fives. Tyler's secretary came flyin' into the office...

"You go girl!"

"You go boy!" I shouted as I gave Tyler a high 5. Jordan picked me up, spun me around, and gave me a big kiss.

"You did good Trenice. I swear you had me worried for a minute."

"Good – that was the whole idea. I knew if you were worried, they were worried."

"We got lucky Trenice – really lucky," Tyler said.

"Girl, when you said I wish your mattress stood like your offer I was on the floor crackin' up!" his secretary laughed.

"That was a good one Trenice," Tyler said as they all laughed.

"I got their fuckin' attention."

"Especially when Gordon said 'appears' and you asked him if he needed fuckin' glasses," Jordan laughed. "I thought you were about to go to jail for assault!"

"Shit – we all did," Tyler laughed.

"The papers should be here next Friday, latest. Have a great day – you earned it."

"We will – and thanks for everything Tyler."

Chapter 30

Once Jordan and I got into the limo I let out a big sigh of relief. "Whew! We did it!"

"You did it Trenice," Jordan said as he pulled me into another kiss.

"And it'll be my pleasure to do it again real soon," I said as I slid down in the seat, pulling Jordan directly on top of me.

"One more week," He moaned in my ear as he continued to kiss me and run his hands up and down my body."

"My pleasure, my pleasure," I moaned, enjoying every minute of it. We were oblivious to the limo driver the entire ride to New York City.

We spent the whole day dinning and shopping, courtesy of MasterCard, Visa, American Express, and Discover.

"At least we won't have to worry about how we're gonna pay these bills next month," Jordan said as we both laughed. I had been oblivious to the pain in my ankle until we sat down for an early dinner. Jordan noticed me rubbing my lower leg.

"You alright Trenice?"

"I'll be ok – I guess I over did it a little."

"After we eat let's get you home. You don't need to re-injure your foot just when the cast is ready to come off."

"You're right."

We finished our meal, dessert, and Jordan wrapped his arm around me as I limped out to the limo. "Wait here – I'll be right back," he said after he put me in the limo. He flew down the street and was back in a few minutes.

"Where'd you go?" Jordan handed me a paper bag from the pharmacy. I looked inside and there was a bottle of ibuprofen – 400 milligrams each.

"Thank you, thank you, thank you," I said as I swallowed two of them on the spot. I stretched out in the back seat as Jordan picked up my feet and placed them in his lap. He rubbed my legs until I fell asleep.

We stopped at Char's house first and gave her the news. "You go girl!" she said as we high-fived each other laughing. "I can't believe it – I would'a took the $20,000 and ran" Char said.

"I almost did – but then I thought about everything I went through and Jordan's grandmother told me not to accept their first offer."

"She did?"

"Yep. She said you never take the first offer – if they offer you twenty, they can go as high as fifty."

"No shit – you got $50,000?!"

"No they didn't go that high."

"How much did you get?"

Jordan and I looked at each other.

"Well?" Char asked.

"We got $600,000," I said.

"Oh my God! What are you gonna do with all that money?"

"I'm gonna put it in a trust fund so I can't fuck it up," I said real quick. "Well, I've had a long day Char, so I'm gonna go."

"Alright girl – your cast comes off next week right?"

"Right," Jordan answered with a mischievous grin.

"Oh shit – it's about to be on ain't it?"

"My pleasure," I laughed as we went downstairs.

When we got to Jordan's house I said, "Can we go see my mother first?"

"You sure you up to it?"

"Yea."

"Ok – let's go." I started 'thumping' upstairs and Miss April opened the door...

"That you Trenice?"

"Yea Mum – we goin' upstairs – we'll be down in a few," Jordan said.

"Ok," she said as she closed her door. When we got upstairs my brothers and sisters were waiting.

"We heard you 'thumpin' up them steps," they laughed as they opened the door.

"Mom, Trenice and Jordan are here," Marlowe said as we sat in the kitchen.

"Hi Trenice, Hi Jordan – how'd it go today?"

"I took the settlement Mom."

"You did?" she asked. As she looked at me Jordan gave me a look too, but no one noticed. Then he caught on...

"Yea, she figured she better take it while it was on the table before they changed their mind."

"Good idea Trenice – no sense in being greedy – be grateful for what you can get."

"Ma, I've had a long day and my ankle hurts so I'm gonna go ok?"

"Ok – take care."

"Bye everybody," I said as I left.

"Bye Trenice, Jordan," they said. I 'thumped" downstairs to Jordan's house.

"You didn't ask for more money?" Miss June asked as we told her we settled.

125

"No Miss June – she was a real bitch – oh excuse my language Miss April, Miss June."

"That's ok honey," Miss April said.

"Well I still think you should'a asked for more, but it's over with now."

Before Jordan could say anything I said, "Well, I better go get off this foot."

"We'll see you later Mum-Mum."

"Ok – get home safe," Miss April said.

"Congratulations," Miss June said."

"Thanks – good night."

"You don't want anybody to know how much money we really got, do you?" Jordan asked as we got in the limo.

"They'll find out soon enough – besides we haven't even got the check yet – we don't need anyone telling us how to spend it."

"True."

Soon as we got to Grandma's house we got upstairs without seeing anyone. We thought we were in the clear until we got in the house.

"Trenice, your lawyer called. He said to tell you the checks would be ready Friday afternoon. How much did you get?" Grandma asked. Damn! Bad enough Aunt Trudy wouldn't let me get a word in, but her nosy ass friend, Sissy was sitting right there all smiles waiting for an answer, along with my grandmother.

"I won't know until he takes his fees out. I'll probably end up with a couple thousand."

"Damn that's it?" Aunt Trudy asked.

"Yea well, lawyers are expensive, and besides — I gotta pay for all these clothes," I said pointing at the bags.

"Well something's better than nothing, but I hope you didn't spend it all before you got it."

"Me too Aunt Trudy."

"Alright Ma — we'll see you later."

"Ok Trudy."

When they left she said, "How much money are you gettin' Trenice? Really?"

"I really won't know until next week Grandma." I didn't lie to her but I wasn't about to tell her either.

"I'll see ya soon Trenice — you look tired," Jordan said.

"I am Jordan," I said as I kissed him good night.

"One more week," he whispered.

"My pleasure," I whispered back.

"I love you."

"I love you too."

Chapter 31

Jordan and I had been talking back and forth on the phone since last Sunday but I hadn't seen him. I missed him so much it hurt. I couldn't believe I was finally on my way to get this cast off. When I got to White Plains Hospital, I didn't have to wait long.

"C'mon in Trenice, Dr. Campton said as I 'thumped' into the office. He laughed as he helped me up on the table. "So far it looks good," he said as he cut the cast off. He picked up my foot and examined it as I wiggled my toes. "Trenice, I'm going to send you for another x-ray just to make sure your foot has healed properly. If all looks good, you can go home, but don't wear any heels for another two weeks. There might be a little tenderness but a few ibuprofens should take care of that.

"Thank you Dr. Campton."

"Trenice?"

"Yes Dr. Campton?"

"Stay away from the Holiday Inn," he laughed as he closed the door. I waited for a few and the technician escorted me to the radiology department. He looked down and saw I had on my sneakers.

"Oh – you walkin' on your foot already?"

"Yea – it's ok."

"Well you're probably fine, but let's get a look at your x-ray to make sure."

"Ok." After I had the x-ray the technician looked it over.

"You're fine Trenice – I'll send this up to Dr. Campton. Have a good day."

"Thanks," I said as I made a beeline outta there.

When I got to Yonkers I went straight to Jordan's job. "You got the cast off – it looks good! You sure you're ok?"

"Yes – I'm fine – I feel like my old self."

"What did the doctor say?"

"He said no heels for another two weeks, take ibuprofen for pain, and stay away from the Holiday Inn." All his co-workers laughed.

"Alright Bob – we out," Jordan said as we went towards the exit.

"I guess I gotta deal with that when I go back to work," I said as we got in the cab.

"I guess you do," Jordan said as he got in beside me.

When we got to Tyler's office, everyone was all smiles. "C'mon in Jordan, Trenice," Tyler said as he escorted us into his office. When we sat down he popped a bottle of champagne, poured 3 small cups, and we toasted to our success.

"Here's to us," we all said. Tyler handed Jordan and I a check for $50,000 each. After he took $150,000, we had Tyler purchase 4 tickets for an all-expense-paid two-week cruise to Bermuda for Miss April, Miss June, my mother, and my grandmother. They would all go on the cruise at the same time – the ship was leaving from New York City the 2nd week of October. We also had Tyler purchase 3 tickets for an all-expense-paid 7 day/6 night cruise to the Bahamas for Char, Jake, and Rachel, including tickets for Amtrak to Florida so they would be able to connect directly to their cruise ship. Jordan and I got round-trip airfare and hotel accommodations for 2 weeks in Hawaii for next year. The rest of the money was put into a joint checking account.

"Thanks again for everything Tyler. We couldn't have done it without you."

"My pleasure Trenice, my pleasure." Jordan and I both looked at each other. Tonight was the night. "And if you ever need me again, my door's always open." "Thanks again Tyler," I said as we left his office. I had no idea we would need his services again so soon.

Chapter 32

"Why don't we go to Jake and Rachel's house? We haven't seen them in a while," I said.

"Good idea," Jordan said as we walked to their house. When we got to their house, Rachel noticed right away...

"Your foot! The cast is gone! When did you get it off?"

"Earlier today."

"So what's been goin' on with the law suit?" Jordan and I looked at each other. He pulled the tickets out of his jacket and handed them to Jake.

"Oh wow honey – we're goin' to the Bahamas!"

"Oh my God – le'me see!"

"Oh my God – Oh my God," she screamed as they jumped up and down hugging.

They pulled us into the hug and I yelled, "Watch the foot!" as we all bust out laughing.

"So when did this get settled," Rachel asked.

"Last week – you should'a been there – I almost went to jail!"

"Oh my God what happened?" I let Jordan tell them. We were all laughing so hard we were holding our stomachs.

"Girl you are crazy," Jake said.

"Yea I had to get up a few times – I thought Trenice was gonna put her cast in that man's ass!" Jordan said. We hollered some more.

"Well, we gotta get goin," I said. "Where y'all goin'?" Jake teased.

"I know it's not the Holiday Inn," Rachel said. We all laughed.

When we got to Char's house and gave her the tickets she grabbed us both jumping up and down screaming, "Thank you – thank you –thank you!"

"You're welcome," Jordan laughed.

"Does your Grandma know yet?"

"No - we goin' to tell her now," I said.

"Alright I gotta work tonight so I'll talk to y'all later. Thank you – I love you," she yelled as we went downstairs.

"I love you too Char," I yelled back.

When we got to Grandma's house she had been waiting on us along with Aunt Trudy and Sissy. "Where you been all day Trenice? Oh my God – your cast is gone! You been takin' it easy on that foot right?"

"Yes Grandma."

"Hi Miss Gladys, Trudy, Sissy."

"Hi Jordan," they said.

"Grandma come upstairs – we got something for you." I might as well have invited Aunt Trudy and Sissy upstairs too 'cause they came right along with us. When we got in the house I gave my Grandma the envelope. She looked at the tickets and started to cry.

"Watcha go and do this for?" she said as she gave me a hug.

"Because I love you Grandma and you deserve it."

"Does your mother know yet?"

"No I'm going to give her her ticket when we leave here.

"What's the ticket for?" Aunt Trudy asked.

"Me and Claire are going to Bermuda for 2 weeks Trudy!" she beamed.

"Oh that's nice," Aunt Trudy said. I could tell she was disappointed.

"Yes that is nice Miss Gladys," Sissy said. "So what you do with the rest of your money?"

"I put it away. Grandma, we gotta go so we see ya later ok?"

"Ok Trenice." We left Aunt Trudy and Sissy sitting in the kitchen with Grandma.

When we got in the cab, Jordan pulled me close to him, kissed me, and whispered, "Tonight."

"My pleasure," I whispered back.

When we got to my mother's house, Bunny answered the door. "Mommy Trenice doesn't have the cast on anymore!"

"Come on in Trenice, Jordan."

"Mom sit down. I have something for you." She sat down and we handed her the envelope as my brothers and sisters watched her open it. Her eyes got wide and she jumped up. "Hott damn – I'm going to Bermuda!"

"Mommy where's Bermuda?" Bunny asked.

"Mommy's going on vacation honey."

"Ohhh – can I go? Please?"

"No Bunny – not this time."

"But I wanna go, I wanna go," she cried.

"Bunny?"

"Yes Trenice?" "How 'bout next week you go to Great Adventure?"

"Really?" she perked.

"Yes."

"Oh yea!" she said as she hugged me.

"Trenice don't have her waitin' if you not gonna take her."

"Oh I figured you were gonna take her Mom."

"Oh I guess you figured you were buyin' us tickets then?"

"Sure Mom." Since I volunteered it I guess it was the least I could do. "Mom we gotta go downstairs and see Miss April and Miss June ok?"

"Ok – I'll see y'all later."

"By Miss Claire," Jordan said.

"Bye Jordan."

When we got downstairs and knocked on the door Miss April was surprised. "No more cast I see – when you get it taken off?"

"I had it taken off this morning Miss April – Hi Miss June."

"Sit down Mum-Mum – we got something for ya." They both stared as Jordan handed them the envelope. When then realized what it was, they jumped up and down screaming, "We goin' to Bermuda – we goin' to Bermuda!"

Just then, there was a knock at the door. I'll get it," I said as I opened the door.

"Is Jordan here?"

"Who are you?" I asked.

"I'm Rosalind."

Chapter 33

"Who is it Trenice?" Jordan asked as he came to the door. When he saw it was Rosalind, his whole expression changed. "What do you want?!" he snapped.

"We need to talk Jordan. Alone."

I wasn't going to disrespect Miss April's house so I kept quiet but, "Bitch, who the fuck do you think you are," was right on the tip of my tongue.

"Rosalind we don't have anything else to talk about. This is Trenice," he said as he pulled me close to him.

"I'm sorry Jordan but we really do need to talk – just for a few minutes...please. That's all I ask." Before Jordan could answer, Miss April and Miss June came to the door. "Hi Miss April, hi Miss June."

"What are you doing here Rosalind?" Miss April asked.

"I need to speak to Jordan. It's important."

"Trenice, I'll be right back ok?"

"No it's not fuckin' ok!" I thought. But what else could he do? "Sure honey."

"You'll be here when I get back?"

"Of course!" No way was I leaving until I heard what that bitch had to say to my man...

"Ok then," he said as I watched him leave with Rosalind.

Just then I got a really uneasy feeling in the pit of my stomach and ran for the bathroom..."Ugh!!"

"Trenice, you alright?!" Miss April called to me in the bathroom. I broke out in a cold sweat. I couldn't go back at there just yet.

"I'm ok Miss April. Must'a been something I ate." When I came out the bathroom, Jordan was just coming in the door.

"What did she want Jordan?!" Miss April snapped. I guess Miss April liked her about as much as I did.

"Mum-Mum I can't talk about this right now. Trenice, can you stay with me a while?"

"Of course." Jordan pulled me close to him, put his head on my shoulder, and Miss April and Miss June stood there in shock as Jordan cried. I held him and let him cry without saying a word. Anger was building up inside me as I thought, "What the fuck did this bitch do to him?" I was scared and angry at the same time. When he stopped crying, Miss April and Miss June came over to him and hugged him. Neither of us said a word.

"Mum-Mum we'll be back later ok?"

"Ok," Miss April said. Jordan took my hand and we went downstairs. We walked until we got to the park.

Chapter 34

Jake and Rachel were waiting for us when we got to the park. "What's up Jordan? What'd she say?" they asked. We all sat own on the bench...

"Fuckin' bitch! I don't fuckin' believe this shit!" he yelled as he punched the bench so hard he scared me.

"What Jordan – what?" Jake asked.

"Now she wanna tell me she made a fuckin' mistake! She and Steven broke up. She found out that Steven's not her baby's daddy – I am – And get this – she wants us to get back together – she claims she still loves me – can you believe that shit?!

"Oh my God!" Rachel screamed.

"Yo man – that's some fucked up shit," Jake said.

"What if it's true? I wanna be a part of my son's life but I don't want anything to do with her – she has the nerve to tell me she still loves me after she ended our marriage to be with that punk ass motherfucker – I hate that bitch!" he yelled as he pounded his fist into the bench.

"It's gonna be alright man," Jake tried to console him but Jordan jumped up,

"How the fuck is it gonna be alright?!!...I'm sorry Jake I don't mean to take it out on you," he said as he slumped back down on the bench and put his head in his hands...

"Its ok man – don't worry about it...."

"I don't think it's yours," I said. They all looked at me in disbelief.

"What makes you say that Trenice?" Jordan asked.

"Think about it. The first time she got pregnant, she told you she wasn't ready for a baby. Then she got an abortion without discussing it with you. If she thought there was a chance this baby was yours, she never would have asked you for a divorce to go be with Steven. Now she's telling you she loves you and she wants to get back together. If you went back to her and re-married her, even if the child isn't your biological child, she would be guaranteed alimony and child support." Everyone was quiet for a minute...

"Fuckin' bitch!" Jordan yelled as he pounded his fist into the bench again.

"Jordan, she may be right," Jake said.

"But how can I prove it? Jordan asked. "I won't know until the baby's born!"

"You tell her you don't think it's your baby. She will take you to court. You won't have to pay for the paternity test because you're denying the child." I said.

"But what if it is mine Trenice? What are we gonna do?"

"We'll get through it together Jordan."

Jordan grabbed me by the face and said, "I love you," as he pulled me into a kiss.

"I love you too."

Chapter
35

I called Char when I got home.

"I can't believe she tryin' to pull some shit like that," Char said. "I bet you right – it probably ain't even his."

"But what if it is his Char?"

"You gonna stay with him?"

"Like white on rice!" I laughed. "So how's your love life Char?"

"Girl, it's better than ever. His divorce is final in two weeks. I'm takin' him on that cruise you gave me."

"I'm glad you're so happy Char."

"Me too girl – me too."

"Well, I gotta go girl, I've had a long, long day."

"Alright girl, keep me posted."

"I will Char."

Grandma came down the hall and saw me sitting at the table crying. "What's wrong Trenice?" I told her all about Rosalind and what I thought. "Oh my poor baby," Grandma said as she hugged me and I cried some more. "Don't you worry – it'll all work out. You love him right?"

"Hell yea! – Oh sorry Grandma."

"He loves you?"

"Yea!"

"Then that's all you need..."

The phone startled us both..."Hello?"

"Trenice, I just got off the phone with Rosalind. She's hot right about now."

"Too fuckin' bad – oh sorry Gramdna – you two would still be married if it weren't for the shit she did to you."

"Yea, she's takin' me to court just like you said she would."

"Good – then this will get settled the right way."

"Yes it will. I told Mum-Mum what happened. My grandmother told your mother. I hope that's alright."

"Sure it is – I was gonna tell her anyway."

"I'll talk to you soon Trenice. I love you."

"I love you too."

Chapter 36

I went back to work on Monday. Everyone was glad to see me. They had a 'Welcome Back' banner and a cake with a bed and some little person lying in the bed with a cast on. The bed was cracked in half. "I'm never gonna live this down," I said to myself.

Jordan came to pick me up from work like he used to. He showed me court papers he had received in the mail.

"Bitch doesn't waste any time does she?" I asked.

"I guess not."

"Jordan she had these papers filed before she talked to you. She came to see you on

Saturday and you get papers today. She probably filed them last week."

"She probably did Trenice."

We went to get dinner and walked to Carvel for dessert. It was nice to be able to walk again. We met Jake and Rachel at the park and Jordan told them about the papers.

"She filed them shits last week," Rachel said.

"We wanna be there when you go to court," Jake said.

"I want you to be there," Jordan said.

When I got home I told Grandma about the papers and what I thought.

"You're probably right Trenice." I didn't see Aunt Trudy standing there.

"Why you buttin' into this Trenice? You have nothing to do with it." Grandma and I spun around...

"Whatchu mean she has nothing to do with this?"

"She doesn't Ma – its's between Rosalind and Jordan – she should mind her own business."

I was so mad I was about to say something but Grandma handled it for me..."Trudy, Rosalind may be your friend but what Rosalind did was fucked up! I'm glad Trenice is telling Jordan what to do and standing by him."

"I gotta go Ma – bye!" she said as she slammed the door.

"I don't give a damn if she is mad Trenice – you did the right thing."

"Thank you Grandma. Hello?" I asked as I answered the phone.

"Trenice, this is Tyler returning your call. How's everything?"

"Not so good Tyler." I explained everything that was going on.

"You did the right thing by calling me Trenice. He shouldn't show up in court without an attorney. Has he thought about what he's going to do if the child turns out to be his?"

"He's going to do the right thing Tyler."

"I'll see ya tomorrow Trenice."

"See ya tomorrow."

Chapter

37

We went to see Tyler first thing Tuesday morning. "I'm glad Trenice called me Jordan. It wouldn't look good for you to show up without an attorney – especially if the child turns out to be yours. I went over all the papers. Have you had your blood test yet?"

"We're going as soon as we leave here," Jordan said.

"Good. Re-read your statement and make sure you didn't leave anything out."

Jordan read the statement over and handed it back to Tyler. "It looks good," he said as he handed him back the papers.

"Ok – I'll talk to you next week."

"Thanks again Tyler," I said.

"My pleasure," Tyler said.

Jordan and I looked at each other and left without saying a word. We never had that night.

When we got to the hospital we went to the lab for the blood test. As we were going in, Aunt Trudy and Rosalind were coming out of the lab. We all just looked at each other. "Hi Aunt Trudy," I said. She just walked right past me like she didn't hear me, along with Rosalind. Oh well. I sat and waited while they took Jordan's blood.

"The court will get these results in 48 hours," the nurse said. Perfect. We were due back in court on Friday.

We met Jake and Rachel in the park later that evening. "She walked right past Trenice like she didn't even see her," Jordan told Jake.

"Don't even worry about it Trenice," Rachel said.

"I don't really care about my Aunt Trudy – I just want us to get this over with so Jordan and I can get back to our lives."

"I want that too Trenice," Jordan said.

When I got home my mother was there and so was Aunt Trudy. "Hi Mom, hi Aunt Trudy."

"Hi Trenice," my mother said.

"Trudy you have no business treatin' Trenice like that," Grandma said.

"I gotta go," she said as she slammed the door.

"Don't worry about her Trenice – she'll get over it," my mother said.

"Mom, all I want is for this to be over so Jordan and I can get back to our own lives."

"What if the child is his Trenice?"

"Then we have a child Mom." She and Grandma smiled at each other.

"I gotta get goin' Ma. – I'll see ya soon. Don't forget those tickets Trenice – Bunny's been buggin' me ever since you brought it up."

"The tickets were mailed to you Ma – you should get them by this weekend."

"Oh ok – bye Ma," my mother said as she hugged Grandma.

"Bye Claire."

"Hang in there Trenice," she said as she hugged me. It had been a long time since my mother hugged me and I needed it.

"I love you Ma."

"I love you too Trenice… I'm so proud of you." Tears came to my eyes. My mother hasn't said that to me since I was a child.

"Cut it out Trenice," she said as she hugged me again. We both laughed.

When my mother left I called Char to give her the latest. "How the fuck is your aunt gonna get mad and not speak to you 'cause his ex-wife is a hoe? Fuckin' stupid bitch!"

"I know – I don't understand it either – it's not like I'm telling Jordan anything wrong – she even gets mad when my Grandma tells her she ain't right."

"What's she gonna do when this is over? I know that's her friend, but you're her niece."

"Well she doesn't see it like that Char. But the only one I really care about is Jordan. This is tearing him up inside."

"When do you go back to court?"

"We go on Friday." I said. "Well le'me go — we gotta get up in the morning."

"Alright I'll talk to ya later," Char said.

"Bye."

Chapter 38

It took forever for Friday to get here. I got up early and went to Jordan's house. "Hi Trenice, come on in," Miss April said as she opened the door. It was a house full. Miss April, Miss June, Jake, Rachel, my mother, Jordan, and I were squeezing past each other. Jordan grabbed me and gave me a hug.

"I love you Trenice."

"I love you too Jordan. No matter what happens, you got me."

We started kissing and Miss April said, "Y'all don't have time for that – we gotta get goin'." We all went downstairs and my mother got in the cab with Jordan and I – Miss April and

Miss June got in the car with Jake and Rachel. When we pulled up in front of the court house, Char was standing there waiting for us.

"Thanks for coming Char," Jordan said.

"You know I was comin'," she said she hugged us both.

"Nice to see you again Char," my mother said.

"Good morning Miss Claire," Char said.

"Char, this is Miss April and Miss June – Jordan's grandmother and Jordan's mother," I said as I introduced them.

"C'mon Mum-Mum," Jordan said to them as we all got in the elevator and went upstairs.

When we got upstairs Tyler was waiting for us. "Tyler this is Miss April, Miss June, my mother Claire, my best friend Char, and Jordan's best friends Jake and Rachel. Just then Grandma came out the ladies room...

"Grandma!" I shouted.

"You didn't think you was gonna be here without me did you?" she said as she hugged me.

"Tyler this is my grandmother Gladys."

"Pleased to meet you Gladys – lets go inside."

When we got inside we saw Rosalind. Her attorney was none other than that fuckin' bitch, Bernice Thomas – the same one that represented the Holiday Inn with Gordon Smith. We all stood there for a minute...

"Everyone, this is Bernice Thomas – she's one of the attorneys that represented the Holiday Inn at my hearing," I said. Everyone bust out laughing.

Tyler smiled and said, "Nice to see you again Bernice." She went inside with Rosalind without responding.

Aunt Trudy and her nosy ass friend, Sissy, came off the elevator. "What the fuck is Sissy doing here?" I thought to myself..."Char, this is my Aunt Trudy and her friend Sissy."

"Nice meeting you," Char said. Neither one of them spoke.

The court officer came out..."Rosalind Williams vs Jordan Williams," she announced. We all went into the court room. Bernice, Rosalind, Aunt Trudy, and Sissy sat on the left. We all sat on the right. After all the swearing-ins and the testimony I sat on the edge of my seat waiting to hear what we came for. Judge Reynolds removed the results from the envelope..."Mr. and Mrs. Williams, will you step forward?" I didn't like that shit. As far as I was concerned, I was Mrs. Williams. "Mr. Williams when it comes to the unborn child, baby Williams...**YOU ARE NOT THE FATHER**." Everyone was quiet. I was happy and sad at the same time. This should have been a happy time for Jordan, but it was anything but...

"You fuckin' bitch! I never should've married you – you put me through all this shit for nothing!"

"Mr. Williams I'm warning you..." Judge Reynolds said.

"Who's the father Rosalind? Do you even know?"

"I'm sorry Jordan... I thought..."

"You tried to fuckin' set me up – I fuckin' hate you!"

"Mr. Williams – one more outburst like that from you and you'll be escorted outta here in handcuffs!" Judge Reynolds yelled.

Tyler put his hand on Jordan's shoulder. "It's over now Jordan. Let it go. It's not worth it."

"Listen to him honey," Miss April said. You don't need to be goin to jail behind this. Let's go home."

I pulled Jordan to me from behind. He turned around and put his head on my shoulder. "We wasted so much time – all for nothing."

"It's over now Jordan – let's just go," I said. Bernice, Aunt Trudy, Sissy, and Rosalind left first. We all left after them. When we got downstairs I said, "I'm hungry – let's go get breakfast."

"Sounds good – sounds good," they all said.

"Tyler you comin' right?" Jordan asked.

"Afraid not – I gotta be back in court later today."

"C'mon Tyler – at least have a cup of coffee," I said. Miss April gave him a 'don't even try and say no' look.

"Ok, but just coffee," he said. We had a good breakfast but Jordan was quiet. After we finished breakfast Jake and Rachel offered to take Miss April, Miss June, and my mother home, but they decided to walk because it was such a nice day. Tyler had his cup of coffee with us and left about ½ hour ago so it was Jake, Rachel, Jordan, my grandmother, and me. Char had to go to work and Jake and Rachel had already made plans so they offered to take Grandma home.

When they were leaving I asked Grandma, "Do you think Aunt Trudy will ever speak to me again?"

"Only time will tell Trenice," she said.

"Alright – see ya later – we gotta get goin'," Jake said.

I gave Grandma a hug and a kiss, helped her in the car, and went back in the diner with Jordan.

We sat at the booth and Jordan didn't say anything.

"You ok honey?"

"I guess. I just can't believe she put me through all that. I loved her so much. I just don't get it. And there was a chance that was my child. I actually was prepared for that. I didn't want to believe that she was sleeping with someone else too. I thought Steven was the only one. In a way, I wanted you to be wrong – in a way I wanted that child to be mine so I wouldn't see my marriage for what it really was – nothing. Does that make sense Trenice?"

I took his hand, placed it in mine, and said, "It makes perfect sense."

We decided to walk back to Grandma's house. When we got upstairs, we could hear Aunt Trudy and Sissy inside...

"I bet she real happy now," Aunt Trudy said.

"She and Jordan probably somewhere celebratin' talkin' 'bout how stupid we are," Sissy said.

"I just can't believe Rosalind went out like that. I just knew Jordan was the father. I actually feel sorry for her. You know what Sissy?"

"What Trudy?"

"When Jordan first started seeing Trenice, I didn't know he was divorced. I told Trenice he was married and I worked with his wife. Here I was tryin' to protect Trenice from him and the whole time, he needed to be protected from Rosalind." They laughed along with my Grandma. A funny feeling came over me. I had just heard my Aunt Trudy say she was tryin' to protect me. I opened the door and went inside...

"Thank you Aunt Trudy – I love you," I said as I gave her a hug."

"What was that for?" she asked. Even Sissy and Grandma Looked perplexed.

"For being you Aunt Trudy. For being you." Grandma smiled at me and nodded. She was right. Or so I thought...

"Hello Trudy, Sissy," Jordan said as I went down the hall to change.

"Hello Jordan," they said.

I smiled to myself. "This is gonna be a good day after all," I thought. When I came back out into the living room, I had a brown suitcase with a few things in it.

"Watcha got in the suitcase?" Sissy asked.

"A little bit o' this – a little bit o'that," I said.

"You got a nightie in there Trenice?" Grandma asked as we all laughed. If she only knew...

"See ya later Grandma, bye Aunt Trudy, by Sissy."

"Bye Miss Gladys, Trudy, Sissy," Jordan said.

"Trenice?"

"Yes Grandma?"

"Should I put the chain on the door tonight?"

Jordan and I looked at each other. Aunt Trudy and Sissy looked at me, waiting for my answer. "Yes Grandma." Jordan looked at me and smiled. We left without saying another word.

When we got downstairs I told Jordan, "When you get home, pack your bag – I'm kidnapping you for the weekend."

"Sounds like a plan," he said as we made a beeline to his house. When we got upstairs Miss April opened the door. "I was wondering if I was gonna see you tonight," she said as Jordan began to hurry around the house, packing an overnight bag.

"Where y'all goin'," Miss June asked.

"Well we know they' not goin' to the Holiday Inn," Miss April said as we all laughed. Jordan zipped up his bag and gave them both a kiss goodbye.

"See you Sunday Mum-Mum."

"Monday," I corrected. Miss April and Miss June looked at us then at each other.

"See you Monday," he said as we left.

"Bye Miss April, Bye Miss June," I said on the way downstairs. Soon as we got downstairs and outside we ran smack into my mother, Marlowe, and Bunny.

"Hi Trenice!" she yelled as she hugged me. "I had sooo much fun today! Where you goin' Trenice?" She was almost sad.

"I'm going on vacation Bunny." She began to pout. "Oh boy," I thought to myself. "This is the last thing I need." Thank God she didn't start crying.

"I'll miss you Trenice. You comin' back?"

"Yes, Bunny I'll be back."

"You promise?"

"Of course."

"Okay. Trenice?"

"Yes Bunny?"

"Thank you for the tickets."

"You're welcome Bunny."

"Good night Miss Claire, Marlowe, Bunny," Jordan said.

"Good night," they all said as they went into the building.

Jordan grabbed me and pulled me into a kiss. "Tonight," he whispered.

"My pleasure," I whispered as we headed toward the train station. I looked back and tapped Jordan on the shoulder. "Look up there," I said as I pointed. We laughed as we noticed that Miss April and Miss June and been looking out the window the whole time.

Chapter 39

We got to the train station and caught the last Amtrak leaving the station. When I showed the conductor our tickets we were escorted to our sleeper.

"What time will we be arriving?" I asked.

"Let's see – you're going to Niagara Falls – about 8 a.m."

"Thank you," I said as Jordan took down the sleeper.

"Niagara Falls huh?" He didn't know where we were going and I couldn't keep it from him for 8 hours. The dining car was open so we went to get something to eat and sat at the table enjoying the scenery as we sped through the cities. I brought along my camcorder and while we were at the table we recorded bits of scenery, people walking back and forth, and on the way back to our sleeper, I recorded a man holding his baby girl. Both of them were sleeping so soundly I couldn't resist. His daughter was cradled in his arms and he was propped up against the window, stretched out in the seat. Jordan waited patiently while I recorded about a minute of this then he followed me back to our sleeper. Once we got inside, I set up the tripod for the camcorder and plugged it in using the outlets provided by Amtrak. I hit the record button and positioned the camcorder so you could record directly out the window, but you could also record directly what was in front of the camcorder. Jordan smiled to himself as he realized we would be directly in front of that camera. I pulled out my portable CD player and, to his surprise; I was singing the song I wrote, 'Sexy Chocolate,' to him through the speakers. We didn't speak as we undressed and I stood in front of the window. Jordan came up to me, we embraced each other, and we began exploring each other's mouths and bodies as the 1st verse of my song came through the speakers:

"Never felt this way before and I'm not ashamed. Everyone around can see you're the one to blame. Wrap your arms around me darling I'm in ecstasy. Tonight I want us to create the perfect fantasy."

I began kissing and sucking on Jordan's nipples and I continued kissing and sucking my way down his body as the change played through the speakers:

"I'm gonna take you and I hope that your prepared. 'Cause where were goin' can never be compared. I want you and I know that you want me. When we get together, we'll make history because you're..."

By the time the chorus was playing through the speakers I was on my knees and I had turned Jordan sideways so I could re-in-act what I did to him in the Jacuzzi and we could record it. I continued to lick and suck his cock as the chorus played through the speakers:

"Sweeter than a sugar plum – Sexy Chocolate
And I'm gonna get me some – Sexy Chocolate
Sweeter than a lollipop – Sexy Chocolate
Tasty down to the last drop – Sexy Chocolate"

Jordan picked me up and pulled me into a deep passionate kiss as the 2nd verse played through the speakers. Without pulling away, he lifted me up and placed me on the sleeper on my back:

"Looking forward to the time we can be alone. Hurry – come to me my love – disconnect the phone. Hunger for your touch my darling – I'm filled with desire. You ignite this passion – now come put out the fire."

As the change repeated, he repositioned the camera and climbed on top of me, kissing, licking, and sucking my earlobes, my neck, my breasts, my nipples, my stomach, and my hips:

"I'm gonna take you and I hope that your prepared. 'Cause where were goin' can never be compared. I want you and I know that you want me. When we get together, we'll make history because you're…"

He continued his pace back and forth on my body from my neck to my breasts, to my nipples, to my stomach, and back down to my hips as the chorus played again:

"Sweeter than a sugar plum – Sexy Chocolate
And I'm gonna get me some – Sexy Chocolate
Sweeter than a lollipop – Sexy Chocolate
Tasty down to the last drop – Sexy Chocolate"

When the 3rd verse began to play, Jordan did as the song instructed. "Allow me to give you your 2nd," he said as he lowered himself between my thighs, grabbed my hips, and worked my lips…

"My pleasure," I moaned as I began to tremble and call out his name. He held firm to my hips and literally rode them as wave after wave of orgasmic pleasure rippled through my body throughout the third verse:

"Pull me closer to your body wanna taste your lips. Lay me down and work it baby – grab hold of my hips. Slide yourself between my thighs – right where I want it. Give me every inch of your Sexy Chocolate."

When the change repeated, he gave me what we'd both been waiting for for so long. "Allow me to give you your 3rd," he said as he slid his cock inside me.

"My pleasure," I moaned as I felt every inch of his cock inside me down to his balls:

"I'm gonna take you and I hope that your prepared. 'Cause where were goin' can never be compared. I want you and I know that you want me. When we get together, we'll make history because you're..."

Our bodies rocked back and forth in unison to the chorus:

"Sweeter than a sugar plum – Sexy Chocolate
And I'm gonna get me some – Sexy Chocolate
Sweeter than a lollipop – Sexy Chocolate
Tasty down to the last drop – Sexy Chocolate"

As the chorus continued to play I wrapped my legs around him, pulled him closer, and our tongues explored each other's mouths as we continued to rock back and forth in unison:

"Sweeeeeettt – Sexy Chocolate
Feels so good to me baby – Sexy Chocolate
Tasty, and sexy – Sexy Chocolate
And Sweet – Sexy Chocolate
Feels so good to me babaaaaaa – Sexy Chocolate
I like the way you work it – Sexy Chocolate
When you do meeee – feels so good – Sexy Chocolate
To me babaaaaaa – Sexy Chocolate

Give it to me ooover and oooover – Sexy Chocolate
Oh it feels so good to meee – Sexy Chocolate
'Cause I like it – and I love it – Sexy Chocolate
Don't stop it."

We began calling each other's names over and over...

"Jordan,"...

"Trenice,"...

"Jordan,"...

"Trenice,"...

"Don't stop – Don't Stop" I begged...

"I won't – I won't" he moaned as we both rode wave after wave of orgasmic pleasure.

I let myself go and lost all control of my body – it was his instrument to play and when he hit the right spot, it was over... "I'm cumin – I'm cumin – I'm cumin"...

"You cumin baby? You cumin?"...

"Oh yes – don't stop – I'm gonna come – don't stop"...

"I'm cumin with you – I'm cumin with you ‑ I'm cumin with you"...

"Jordan,"...

"Trenice,"...

"Jordan,"...

"Trenice...Oh shit..."

We collapsed in each other's arms and I started to cry softly. "What's wrong baby, don't cry, don't cry... shhhhh...." Jordan didn't realize I was crying tears of Joy.

"I'm ok baby, I'm ok."

"You sure?"

"I'm happy Jordan. For the first time in my life, I'm truly happy." We lay there and continued kissing and holding each other until we heard the timer click off on the camcorder. That was our cue to get some sleep.

Chapter

40

When we got to Niagara Falls on Saturday morning, check in wasn't until 2 p.m. so we checked in our bags and went on an all day cruise which included breakfast and lunch. After a day of site seeing, we were ready to check into the hotel. I had been very specific when I made the reservations and when we got to the room, I was happy to see that they followed my request to the letter. The room was much like the room we had at the Holiday Inn Crown Plaza with a few exceptions:

Instead of a chandelier hanging from the ceiling, there was a ceiling fan. Plush navy blue carpeting soothed our aching feet and white furniture trimmed in powder blue complemented the powder blue walls and carpet. There was a table for two, also white trimmed in powder blue, with chairs to match, and on the table was a bottle of honey, a bottle of chocolate syrup, some cherries, and some whipped cream. Jordan smiled when he saw this. There was a little kitchenette with a dishwasher, refrigerator, and a Jacuzzi in the middle of the room. The walls were mirrored from top to bottom.

The bathroom was powder blue, with white towels trimmed in powder blue with plush navy blue carpeting and a Jacuzzi for 2, including a shower – just like at the Holiday Inn.

We looked in the bathroom and smiled at each other. Jordan pulled me close to him and whispered, "Care to take a shower with me?"

"No not yet," I said with a grin. I had other plans.

Chapter

41

I took Jordan out into bed room and sat him down on the bed. Jordan pulled me on top of him and began exploring my mouth with his tongue. I tried to pull away but Jordan wouldn't let me get up... "Wait Jordan," I whispered.

"I don't wanna wait Trenice," He whispered as we continued kissing.

"I'll make it worth your while... I promise," I whispered as we kissed some more. I got up and pulled Jordan up into the sitting position. "Wait here," I said.

Jordan eyes followed me as I went to open my suitcase. I took out the tripod for the camcorder and set the camcorder up to record.

After pushing the record button, I took out the portable CD player and, to Jordan's surprise; I had taken his tape of slow Jams and copied it on to a CD. I pulled out what looked like an ordinary inflatable mattress. He watched as I put the mattress on the floor and inflated it. When it was fully inflated, he could see this was no ordinary mattress. The top was covered in velvet and there were velvet binds at the bottom for the feet and leather ties at the top for your hands. I also took out a velvet blindfold, some flavored massage oils, and a portable swing, which I laid on the bed.

"I didn't know you were such a freak," Jordan whispered.

"You don't know the half of it," I whispered back.

I turned on the music and as 'Love Won't Let Me Wait' played through the speakers I went over to the bed. "Take off your clothes." Jordan smiled at me and did as he was told. I took him by the hand and we both knelt down in the middle of the mattress. I gently pushed him down on his back. I bound his feet and his hands then I placed the blindfold on him. I opened the cherries and fed one to Jordan, then one to myself. I dripped the honey all over his body and proceeded to lick, suck, and kiss it off, starting from his neck, being slow and deliberate as I worked my way around his nipples, down his chest, his stomach, and down to his cock, which was standing at attention, all the while Jordan was moaning with pleasure. I dribbled some chocolate syrup all over his cock, topped it off with some whipped cream and a cherry, and proceed to enjoy my chocolate sundae. Jordan continued to moan as I kissed, licked, and sucked his cock until it was clean then I proceeded to kiss lick and suck the honey off his thighs and legs. Then I sucked his toes one by one by one. I untied his hands, unbound his feet and he pushed me down on my back. "I'm not finished with you," I whispered. Jordan lifted me up, pulled me close to him and pulled me into a kiss. When he went to remove the blind fold, I whispered, "No leave it on."

"Okay."

"Lay down on your stomach."

Jordan did as he was told. I bound his feet and tied his hands then I got a bottle of strawberry-flavored massage oil and massaged his entire upper body. Jordan moaned with pleasure as I kissed him all over as I was massaging his arms, his shoulders, his back, then I got down to his sexy ass. I laid my face down on his ass and began to kiss his ass all over as I rubbed it down with the strawberry-flavored massage oil. "I've been wanting to do this since the first time I saw your sexy ass," I said as I continued to kiss and massage his ass. Jordan continued to moan with pleasure as I kissed and massaged his thighs and his legs. Once I was done with his legs, I did what I refer to as the '70' - I turned myself on my back and slid myself up underneath him without unbinding him. I placed his cock in my mouth, grabbed his ass with my hands, and squeezed his ass as he began fucking my mouth.

"That's it – suck it baby – suck it – suck my cock – I'm cumin – I'm cumin – I'm cumin..."

When he was finished, I slid out from underneath him, unbound his feet, untied his hands, and removed the blindfold. He got up, turned around, and pulled me down on top of him. He turned me over on my back, pulled my face to his, began exploring my mouth with his tongue, and slid his hand between my thighs. When he found my clit, I squirmed and moaned as he slid his fingers deep inside my pussy, slid his hand back up over my clit, then proceeded to fuck me with his fingers while he had his tongue in the back of my throat. He placed my hands over my head, spread them apart, and tied them to the mattress. Next, he spread my legs and bound my feet to the mattress. He placed the blindfold on me then proceeded to feed me cherries then himself. Jordan dripped honey all over my body and proceeded to lick, suck, and kiss it off, starting at my neck and being more slow and deliberate when he reached my breasts and nipples. He licked, kissed, and sucked on my breasts while turning my nipples in his fingers – first one then the other. I moaned with pleasure has he worked his way down my body – kissing, licking, and sucking on my stomach as he massaged my breasts until he got down to my pussy. I moaned as he licked my clit slowly and deliberately – then he dripped honey on my legs and thighs and kissed, licked and sucked my legs and thighs while he fucked me with his hand. I was bucking and moaning wildly. He removed his fingers from my pussy and kissed the bottom of my feet then he sucked my toes – one by one by one. He lowered himself on top of me and began exploring my mouth with his tongue as he untied my hands then slid himself down between my legs and unbound my feet. He turned me over on my stomach, spread my hands, tied them to the mattress, spread my legs, and tied them to the mattress. He reached for the banana-flavored massage oil and I moaned with pleasure as he massaged my arms, my shoulders, my back, all the while kissing me all over. When he got down to my ass, he massaged it with the massage oil then as he was kissing my ass all over, he slid his hand up underneath me until he found my clit. I moaned even louder as he slid two fingers inside my pussy and fucked me with his fingers as he kissed and licked my ass. He moved across my thighs and down my legs, kissing and massaging them until he got to my feet.

He turned himself on his back, slid his face up under my body, and returned the '70' – he grabbed my ass and squeezed it as he licked and sucked my clit and tongue-fucked me...

"OOOOOOOOHHHHHHHH that feels ssoooooooooo good....don't stop, ohhhhhhhhh that's itttttttttttt......I'm cumin – I'm cumin – I'm cumin..."

He slid out from underneath me and left me tied and bound to the mattress as he filled the Jacuzzi. He looked in the suitcase and found the seashell and the powder blue bath salts and placed some of them in the Jacuzzi. When he untied my hands, unbound my feet, and removed the blindfold, he led me to the Jacuzzi as 'Between the Sheets' was playing through the speakers. We slid into the Jacuzzi and for the next hour, we licked, sucked, and fucked. He slid me down in the water and slid his cock inside me and we bucked back and forth while splashing water all over the tile floor. After another explosive orgasm, we both lay in the Jacuzzi and let the water soothe our bodies until the water began to cool...

"You hungry?" Jordan asked.

"Yes. We've worked up an appetite huh?" I said as we laughed, climbed out the Jacuzzi, cleaned up the water, turned off the camcorder, put on our robes, and ordered room service. We ordered steak, shrimp for me, chicken for him, baked potatoes, string beans, Caesar salad, Pepsi, bottle water for the fridge, and apple crisp with caramel and vanilla ice cream for dessert. While we were eating, we talked about the mattress.

"I really had fun on that mattress." Jordan said.

"Me too."

"Where did you find out about that?"

"Xanadria Catalog. I had ordered it a long time ago. I used to fantasize about what you and I would do to each other on that mattress."

"Here's to a dream come true," Jordan said as he raised his glass to mine.

"Thank you."

"For what?"

"For allowing me to be myself. I've always wanted to experience these things, but I had to repress this part of myself for so long. It feels so good to be able to give you all of me and not hold anything back."

"I couldn't agree more," he said with a mischievous grin. We finished dinner and dessert, cleaned up, and fell asleep holding each other while the television watched us.

Chapter

42

When I woke up Sunday morning, I got up while Jordan was still asleep and I set the camcorder up to record. After pushing the record button, I climbed back in the bed and woke Jordan up by kissing, licking, and sucking his cock.

"Hmmmm...," he moaned as he woke up with his cock in my mouth. I crawled up on top of him.

"Good morning," said as I kissed him and explored his mouth with my tongue. I continued kissing him and grabbed his cock in my hand, massaging it up and down. Jordan removed my hand, turned me on my back, got up off the bed, and stood at the end of the bed.

"Tell me how much you want it Trenice," he said as he began massaging his cock in front of me.

"I want it bad Jordan."

"Say please."

"Please Jordan."

"Please what?" He continued to massage his cock – it looked so good I wanted to suck it...

"Please let me suck your cock." Jordan came over to the other side of the bed and I began sucking his cock again...

"How does it feel Trenice? Tell me how my cock feels in your mouth..."

"I love your cock in my mouth," I said as I continued to lick and suck his cock. "I love the way it feels, I love to lick it, I love to suck it..." Jordan moaned with pleasure for a while then he pulled away...

"You want me to fuck you Trenice?"

"Yes, fuck me," I panted.

"Say please."

"Please fuck me." "Jordan climbed up on top of me and slid his cock inside me...

"How does it feel Trenice?" Tell me how my cock feels in your pussy..."

"Your cock feels so good in my pussy – oohh it feels so good, don't stop..." He continued for a while then he pulled out and we fucked in the following positions:

First, Jordan slid his cock back inside me and fucked me in what I refer to as the **'missionary slope'** – the missionary position with my legs up on his shoulders. Next, Jordan pulled out and slid down to the end of the bed. He backed up until we were ready to get into the next position I refer to as the **'69' twist** – he backed up, placed his cock in my mouth, then while I was sucking his cock he turned his body clockwise and positioned himself to suck my pussy while I sucked his cock, then turned his body clockwise again until his head was at the end of the bed, then turned his body clockwise again and positioned himself to suck my pussy while I sucked his cock. From this position we went without stopping to the **'propeller'** – Jordan turned clockwise around and around and around while I continued sucking his cock. When he got up, I went over to the suitcase, pulled out a box of condoms, and jumped back on the bed...

"What are these for?"

"Freaky shit," I said with a grin. Jordan smiled to himself as he remembered our conversation about anal sex in the park. He put the first condom on and we proceeded to what I refer to as the **'freak up'** – he turned me over on my stomach, pulled me up as if he were going to fuck my pussy doggy style, and fucked me in the ass. I moaned with pleasure as he fucked me for a while then he pulled out, put another condom on, climbed back on the bed, turned me over on my back, and proceeded to what I refer to as the **'freak down'** – he climbed on top of me as if he were going to fuck my pussy in the missionary position and fucked me in the ass some more. I moaned with pleasure as he fucked my ass some more, then he pulled out, removed the condom, took me by the hand, and led me to the wall. We proceeded to what I refer to as **'69' upside down** – I did a hand stand against the wall and he held my body against the wall, slid my body up until his cock was in my mouth, then he ate my pussy while I was sucking his cock upside down against the wall.

We did that for a while then he backed up, let me slide down, turn right side up, lifted me up, and we proceeded to what I refer to as the **'missionary up'** position – he slid my body up on the wall, slid me down on his cock, and held me in that position as I wrapped my legs around his waist and he fucked me standing up while my body was up against the wall. We did that for a while then he backed away and let me slide back down to the floor. We proceeded to what I refer to as the **'wheel barrel'** - I put my hands on the floor and he picked up my body, slid his cock inside me, and held my legs while he fucked me from behind. From this position without stopping we went into what I refer to as the **'butterfly clip'** - as he continued fucking me I clasped my feet behind him, pulling him closer into my body. He let me down and we proceeded to what I refer to as the 'mission accomplished' – I did a half hand stand against the wall, resting my knees on my elbows, facing away from the wall, and he squatted down, sliding his cock inside me, fucking me, while facing the wall. We did that for a while and then he stood up and helped me up. There was only one thing left for us to do...

After we attached the swing to the ceiling, I set the camcorder up to record and Jordan laid me in the swing on my back. We proceeded to what I refer to as the 'missionary swing' – he fucked me in the missionary position while I laid on my back and he was standing up, slamming his cock harder and harder into my pussy, swinging me back and forth. He pulled out, turned me on my stomach in the swing and we proceeded to what I refer to as the 'doggy swing' – he fucked me doggy style from behind while standing up, slamming his cock harder and harder into my pussy...

"Oh shit I'm cumin – I'm cumin, I'm cumin..."

"You cumin baby? I'm cumin with you – I'm cumin with you..."

"Oh shit...AGGHH!!!"

Chapter
43

"Hello Miss Gladys," Jordan said when we got back.

"Hi Jordan – where's Trenice?"

"She's coming in now," he said as he held the door open for me.

"Oh my God Trenice – how in the hell did you break your leg?"   I hobbled in with the crutches as Grandma, my mother, Aunt Trudy, and Sissy looked at us in shock.

"Y'all break another bed Trenice?" Sissy sneered as everyone else laughed.

"What hotel you suin' this time?" They all hollered when my mother asked that question.

"We didn't break any beds and we're not suing anyone," I said as I sat down.

"What happened Trenice?" I had to make this good. Grandma could glare right through you and you had better not so much as flinch – let alone lie! Oh well – here goes....

"Jordan warned me to be careful but you know how stubborn I can be..." Jordan's eyes got wide as quarters and before I could say anything else he jumped in...

"Miss Gladys I can explain..."

"Shut up and let Trenice talk – her mouth works just fine...go ahead Trenice..." Jordan looked at me pleading for me not to tell them with his eyes...

"We went outside at 4:30 a.m. to see the sun come up..."

"Yea?"

"Well it was so pretty I wanted to get a better picture..."

"So?"

"So I told Jordan to hold on to me so I could lean over the bar and get a better picture..."

"What bar Trenice?" Sissy asked ˗ then she got all up in my face. I swear if it wasn't for my grandmother I'da told Sissy to get the fuck outta my face – bad enough Grandma was giving me the 3rd degree in front of this bitch – but she had to be up in my face too?

"Jordan, can you give me that hanger over there? My knee itches..."

"Sure Trenice – here…"

"Whew! Thanks…" I swung my leg up on the couch and kicked that bitch right in the stomach…

"Dammit!"

"Oh my God – I'm sorry Sissy – you ok? I swear – I hate this fuckin' cast – God I wish I listened to you Jordan – I'm really sorry Sissy," I lied with fake tears in my eyes for emphasis as I pretended to scratch my knee…

"That's ok Trenice – let me get up so you can stretch your leg."

Mission accomplished … tee hee hee…"Thanks Sissy. Jordan hand me the pictures we got…" Jordan handed me the pictures looking perplexed as ever…"See this picture Grandma?"

"Yea? So?"

"So Jordan warned me not to lean over this bar here but would I listen? Nooooo – I just had to get the picture – So Jordan held on to me and I leaned over the bar and took the picture…"

"Trenice are you telling me you leaned over this bar? Where the falls are?"

"Yes Grandma."

Grandma popped Jordan upside the head as she said, "You stupid ass – she could've drowned!"

Grandma it wasn't his fault!"

"I don't give a damn whose fault it was Trenice! I swear if you put your brain in a bird, the damn bird would fly backwards! And Jordan why the hell didn't you tell her she was crazy?"

"I'm sorry Miss Gladys."

"You should be... wait a minute...how did you break your leg?"

"I leaned over the bar while Jordan was holding me and took the picture. When I tried to get back up I dropped the camera in the water so I leaned forward to get it..."

"Oh my God!" my mother screamed.

"That's when I slipped over the bar and fell in..." The fake ears were right on cue...

"The only reason I didn't go over the falls and drown is 'cause my leg got caught between the rocks – Jordan was so scared he reached in and yanked me out as hard as he could..."

"Calm down Trenice – the important thing is that you're ok," Grandma said as she hugged me...

"Trenice?"

"Yes Grandma?"

"What did the paramedics say when they came to get you?" Jordan's eyes got wide as quarters again...

"We hobbled back to the hotel, we changed our clothes, and then Jordan drove me to the hospital."

"Why'd you do all that?"

"Well, besides being embarrassed for falling in, we could've gotten a big fine for attempting to go over the falls...they have signs all over the place..."

"Damn Trenice – no one can ever accuse you of living a dull life can they?" Sissy said.

Damn – maybe I shouldn't have kicked Sissy in her stomach – she feelin' all sorry for me 'n shit..."I guess not Sissy," I said with my head down...I added a few more fake tears for emphasis...

"Trenice?"

"Yea Aunt Trudy?"

"You sure that's what happened?"

"Trudy leave her alone!" Grandma said.

"But Ma..."

"Dammit Trudy I said leave her alone!"

"Stop it!" I screamed.

"Now see what you did Trudy? I told ya leave the damn girl alone!"

"Grandma she's not bothering me!" I screamed.

My mother just threw up her hands, shrugged her shoulders, and muttered, "I don't fuckin' believe this shit..." Little did they know I couldn't fuckin' believe this shit...

"What's wrong with you Claire?" Aunt Trudy asked.

"What's wrong with you Trudy? Trenice doesn't have to explain a fuckin' thing to you – and you gonna ask her if she's sure that's what happened – like she would make the shit up..."

"Well it is a little hard to believe Claire..."

"Go to hell Trudy..."

"That's enough you two..." Grandma said.

"See Ma – then you wonder why I don't come over here – everything revolves around your precious little Trenice – the perfect little angel that does no wrong..."

"Oh my God – stop it!" I screamed. "Aunt Trudy what the hell's the matter with you? You really think I would damn near drown myself to get some attention? I swear – I thought we were finished with this bullshit after what happened with Rosalind – damn!" No one said a word. I couldn't believe I actually said that shit!

"C'mon Sissy let's get the hell outta here," Aunt Trudy said as she went out the door. Sissy followed right behind her and let the door slam.

"Don't be slamming my damn door Sissy!" Grandma yelled. Now I was glad I kicked that bitch in the stomach!

"I'm sorry Grandma – this is all my fault."

"No it isn't either Trenice." My mother said. "I don't know what Trudy's problem is Ma – Trenice didn't do a damn thing to her and I sure as hell wasn't gonna sit here and let her call Trenice a liar!"

"No one's expecting you to do that Claire," Grandma said.

"Trenice I gotta get going," Jordan said as he headed towards the door...

"I'm going with you Jordan," I said.

"Trenice you got a cast all the way up your leg – you need to stay off it." Grandma said.

"Grandma we've been sitting for nearly 10 hours – I'll be ok – Jordan will make sure..."

"Oh right – like he made sure your ass didn't fall in the first place." Grandma said sarcastically.

"I'll be back later Grandma," I said as I damn near pushed Jordan out the door into the hallway..."

"I don't fuckin' believe this shit!" Jordan said.

"Hi Sissy!" I said deliberately loud so Jordan would know we weren't alone.

"Hi Trenice – be careful – you don't wanna break the other leg..."

I wanted to tell her shut the fuck up but I didn't..."I sure don't Sissy – see ya later."

"Ok – take care," she said as she went into her apartment and closed the door. "Damn – she bein' all nice 'n shit like she really feels sorry for me..."

"Maybe she does Trenice..." Jordan said.

"Yea right – let's get outta here before...bye Aunt Trudy..."

She walked past us and knocked on Sissy's door. When Sissy opened the door, Aunt Trudy went inside. Jordan sighed and said, "Let's go."

Soon as we got downstairs, as if things weren't bad enough, Tony opens the lobby door. "Hi Tony," I said.

"Hi Trenice – let me get the door for you."

"Good lookin'," Jordan said as we left the building. I was so glad we stopped to rent a car before we got to Grandma's house.

Once we got in the car Jordan asked, "So that's our story?"

"Yes."

"You sure about this?"

"Well we damn sure couldn't tell them the truth!"

"I can't believe they believed you – if I didn't know any better, I'da believed you too!"

"Yea I laid it on pretty thick – I even cried on cue," I laughed.

"Aunt Trudy almost blew yours wide open."

"She damn sure did – I couldn't believe that shit – and Grandma jumped in right on time too."

"You know we can never tell anyone the truth now Trenice."

"It'll be our secret."

"We can't even tell Jake and Rachel – and you sure as hell can't tell Char!"

"I know, I know!"

"You think we can pull this off?"

"We got past Grandma didn't we?"

"We're not outta the woods yet Trenice."

"I can repeat my performance again if I have too."

"Oh you will have too – believe me!"

We stopped at Jake and Rachel's house first. "Not again," they both said as we got outta the car. When we told them the 'story' they were both in shock.

"Oh my God – I would'a left the fuckin' camera in the water!" Rachel said.

"Man I know you was about to shit on yourself when Trenice fell in the falls," Jake said.

"That was nothing compared to Trenice's grandmother. She pooped me upside my head and told me I should'a told Trenice she was crazy!"

"Get the fuck outta here!" Jake said.

When we told them everything that happened Rachel said, "Maybe you should stay away from your Aunt Trudy – she's got some major issues."

"I wish I could Rachel – but Sissy lives right down the hall from Grandma."

"Damn – I forgot about that."

"Well gotta stop and see Char so we'll see ya later," Jordan said.

"Alright – we'll get up later," Jake said.

"That wasn't so bad," Jordan said as we got in the car."

"No it wasn't," I said.

"Trenice?"

"Yea?"

"This is kinda weird – but it's also kinda fun."

"Fun?"

"Yea – keeping our secret."

"Yea – it is kinda fun."

We sat for a moment then I said, "I wonder what Dr. Campton will think?"

"Depends on what you tell him."

"I'm gonna tell him the same thing I'm telling everyone else!"

"Ok, ok Trenice – calm down!"

"I'm sorry. Let's go see Char and get this over with."

"Okay."

When we got to Char's house she was looking out the window. She ran downstairs and came to an abrupt stop when she saw me. "Again Trenice?"

"No, no, no Char – it was nothing like that this time. Let's go upstairs and we'll tell ya what happened," Jordan said. When we got upstairs we told her the whole 'story.' She sat there for a few then she said,

"Yea right."

"Whatchu mean Char?"

"You can tell that story 1,000 times but we all know that's not what happened."

"Char, you think Trenice made this up?" Jordan asked.

"I know she did."

"What makes you say that?"

"Cause I know Trenice better than you think and I know damn well she ain't fall off no bar." Jordan and I looked at each other without saying a word. "So you broke another bed?"

"No Char."

"You sure?"

"Positive."

"Well if you don't wanna tell me that's ok – I'm your best friend – I've always been there for you and I've never betrayed you – you know you can trust me – but that's okay – don't tell me."

"Oh alright already – I fell but it wasn't over the bar – and that's all I'm gonna say." Jordan threw up his hands and looked at me, shaking his head...

"Trenice?"

"Yea?"

"You remember last year when I broke my leg?"

"Yea."

"How do you think I broke my leg?"

"I don't know – I never asked you..."

"What was I doing when I broke my leg?" I thought about it for a minute...

"Oh my God!" I screamed.

"Thaaats riigghht!"

"Char, you broke your leg the same way Trenice broke hers?"

"How else would I know she made it up?"

"I wonder if Aunt Trudy broke her leg too," I said.

"Why would you say that?"

"Char you wouldn't believe it. Trudy started trippin', Miss Gladys jumped in it, Claire and Trudy had words – I swear I don't know what her problem is."

"Jordan, Trudy's been acting like that ever since Trenice started living with her grandmother."

"You should've seen it Char – Claire cursed Trudy out and told her Trenice didn't have to explain a fuckin' thing to her – after it was all said and done she left and Sissy went right behind her and let the door slam!"

"What started all that?"

"She thinks I'm lyin' Char."

"Then Damn!"

"Grandma defended me along with my mother – and the thing that's so fucked up is I said I thought we were through with the bullshit after what happened with Rosalind!"

"Oh I know she ain't speakin' to you now!"

"She's not," I said.

"I swear – Trudy is so fuckin' immature – she just mad 'cause you said that shit!" Char said.

"I know Char."

"You think they believe you?"

"They do Char – even Sissy was feelin' sorry for me and bein' all nice 'n shit!"

"Damn Trenice – what you gonna do about Trudy?"

"It doesn't matter – everyone else believes me and I even showed them pictures to back up my story."

"Damn girl – you good!"

"Yea she's good alright – Grandma popped me upside my head and told me I should'a told Trenice she was crazy!" Jordan laughed.

"Damn Trenice – I hope she never finds out."

"Who the fuck's gonna tell her?" We all bust out laughing.

"So where is it?"

"Where's what?"

"The swing."

"It's in the car Char," Jordan said.

"What if your Mum-Mum's find it?"

"Oh they won't – I lock everything up – I'll just put in with my tapes."

"Well I sure as hell can't bring it to my house!" I yelled as we all bust out laughing.

"Especially with Aunt Trudy on the case – I wouldn't be a bit surprised if she didn't try to call and check on your story," Char said.

"She can call if she wants – she won't get anything," I said.

"Well we gotta get goin' Char – you ready Trenice?"

"Yea – I'm ready."

"See you soon Char," Jordan said.

"Bye freaks," Char said as we went down stairs.

When we got to Jordan's house Miss April started right in…"I thought you were gonna stay away from the Holiday Inn?"

"Y'all never learn do ya," Miss June said as she laughed. We just shook our heads.

"Trenice you alright?" "Yea – I'm ok Miss April – Jordan was actually more afraid than I was."

"Why was Jordan afraid? What happened!"

"Can we sit down for a minute Mum-Mum?"

"Here Trenice – sit down," Miss April said as she pulled out the kitchen chair.

"Now what happened?" Miss June asked as she got up in my face closer than Sissy – damn!

"Jordan, get the pictures…" Thankfully it didn't take much to convince them – it's true what they say – a picture really is worth a thousand words!

"Mum-Mum we gonna go upstairs – we'll be back ok?"

"Alright Trenice – don't you fall down those stairs and break your other leg," Miss April said.

"Alright – I'll be careful," I said as we left to go upstairs.

When we got upstairs my mother answered the door.

"Hi Miss Claire," Jordan said as we went inside.

"Damn – again Trenice?" my mother said as everyone laughed and Marlowe shook his head back and forth.

"Mommy?"

"Yes Bunny?"

"Trenice isn't fat right?" Jordan and I looked at each other then at my mother, then back at Bunny.

"No she isn't Bunny – why do you ask?"

"And Jordan is big but he's not fat either right?"

"No Bunny – why?"

"So why do the beds keep breaking then?"

We couldn't hold it in any longer. Jordan and I were holding our stomachs along with everyone else – my mother dropped the frying pan on the floor and fell back into the table – we were all laughing so hard Bunny interrupted us...

"What's so funny? Why is everyone laughing at me?"

"We're not laughing at you Bunny – we're laughing at what you said."

"I don't get it – a broken bed is funny?" We were doubled over in laughter again...

"Stop laughing at me!"

"Jordan, get the picures..."

After we filled them in Bunny said, "Trenice?"

"Yes Bunny?"

"Can you sleep here from now on?" Everyone got real quiet.

"Bunny I live at Grandma's house."

"Mommy will let you come home – right Mommy?" Oh boy...

"Bunny, Trenice can come home anytime – she's always welcome here."

"Then why does she live with Grandma?"

"Bunny I live with Grandma because she will be all by herself if I don't live there."

"But we can go visit her then she won't be lonely. Aunt Trudy is there. Then you can sleep here and you won't get hurt anymore," she said with tears in her eyes.

"Well I can talk to Grandma about it but right now I need to stay there because of my leg."

"Why Trenice? Mommy can help you – right Mommy?"

"Of course Mommy can help me Bunny – but Mommy has more steps than Grandma."

"Oh so you gonna stay with Grandma so you can walk up the stairs?"

"Yes Bunny."

"Trenice?"

"Yes Bunny?"

"I think that's a good idea."

"You do?"

"Yea – Mommy is always yellin' at me to be careful 'cause I fall when I run up and down the stairs." We all started laughing again.

"Miss Claire I'm gonna take Trenice home now – we'll see you later."

"Oh ok – bye Trenice," she said as she gave me a kiss. "And please be careful."

"I will Mom."

"Trenice?"

"Yes?"

"I love you."

"I love you too – good night everyone!" Bunny damned near knocked me down when she ran up to me and hugged me tight.

"Take it easy Bunny – you almost knocked her down!"

"I'm sorry – you ok Trenice?"

"Of course I am silly – I'll see y'all tomorrow."

When we got back to Grandma's house she opened the door and said, "Both of you sit down here." Jordan looked at me and I shrugged my shoulders as if to say 'I don't know...' "The Quality Inn called." Shit, shit, shit, shit, shit! Jordan's eyes got wide as quarters but I remained cool...

"They did? Already?" Just then, Aunt Trudy and Sissy came walking in and sat down at the table with us – I wanted to knock their asses away from the table, but I knew damn well I couldn't do that...

"Yea – they said they wanted to talk to you about damages in the hotel room? What damages Trenice?" Aunt Trudy and Sissy were all in my face right along with Grandma. And she had that damned glare – the one that dared you to flinch let alone lie!

"I'm not sure – did they leave a number?"

"Trudy, give her the number." Aunt Trudy passed me the paper with a smirk on her face, but I had something for all of them. I picked up the phone and dialed the number and when they answered I asked for the management office.

"This is Trenice Robertson. Yes, that's right. Uh huh. Oh that's nice! Thank you very much!" When I hung up the phone they were all looking at me waiting to pounce..."Honey – guess what?"

"Umm... what Trenice?"

"Well remember when the toilet overflowed and they had to come in the room and replace the towels and stuff and you had to throw your jeans away?"

"Umm... yea... why?"

"Well everyone else that stayed on the same floor as us started complaining and threatened to take them to court – so they're sending us a certificate for a free weekend at the hotel and they're not charging us for the room!"

"They're not?"

"Nope – they wanted me to call them back so I could let them know if we wanted a check or if we wanted them to credit the credit card we used...isn't that great?"

"Yea – I guess it is," Jordan said. Grandma, Sissy, and Trudy just looked at me as if to say 'yea right' but they didn't say anything.

"Ma I gotta go – see ya tomorrow."

"Alright – bye Trudy, by Sissy."

"I gotta get going too – bye Miss Gladys."

"Good night Jordan," she said as she went down the hall.

Jordan pulled me into a deep passionate kiss and whispered in my ear, "That was close…"

I reached in between his legs and whispered, "This is even closer…"

"Ahem!" We both jumped – we didn't even realize Grandma had come back down the hall…good thing she couldn't see what I was doing to Jordan under the table…"I thought you were leaving Jordan?"

"I am Miss Gladys – good night," Jordan said as he got up and left.

After Jordan closed the door Grandma asked, "You want some coffee?"

"Sure Grandma." I sat at the table and watched my grandmother intently – I knew she was thinking and I knew she wanted to ask me something…

"Trenice?"

"Yes Grandma?"

"Never mind – here," she said as she placed the coffee on the table.

"Thanks Grandma."

Chapter 44

First thing I did when I got up was call Ms. Tyree in Payroll. I knew I had to brace myself...

"Again Trenice?"

"Ha ha ha...very funny."

"So how long will you be out?"

"I don't know for sure – I won't know until I go to the doctor."

"Ok – we'll put you out on disability – but make sure you have your doctor fax us a copy of the papers ASAP."

"Ok – will do."

"Trenice?"

"Yes?"

"Try not to break another bed while you're out," she laughed.

"Right now I'm in no condition to break anything – let alone another bed," I said matter-of-factly.

"Yea right Trenice," she laughed.

I hung up the phone and shook my head. "I don't think I'll ever live this down," I said to myself.

"Live what down Trenice?"

"Oh – good morning Grandma."

"Good morning."

"I was just on the phone with Ms. Tyree in payroll."

"Oh boy – I can imagine how that went," Grandma laughed. "She thinks you broke another bed doesn't she?"

"Everyone thinks I broke another bed Grandma."

"Did you?"

"Grandma!"

"Well?"

"Grandma I explained..."

"Trenice, just because I defended you doesn't mean I'm stupid."

"I never said you were stupid!"

"Don't get huffy with me Trenice!"

"Don't call me a liar and I won't get huffy!"

"I didn't exactly call you a liar Trenice..."

"You don't exactly believe me either!" I said as I slammed the door and hobbled down the stairs. When I got to the bottom of the stairs Tony was right there.

"Hi Trenice."

"Hi Tony."

"Let me get the door for you," he said as he opened the door.

"Thanks." Thank God the cab pulled up just as Sissy and Aunt Trudy were coming up the walkway. I got in the cab and slammed the door before they could speak to me – they probably weren't thinking about speaking to me anyway.

When I got to Jordan's house he was coming out the building.

"Can you wait here please?"

"Ok, but don't be too long – time is money."

I got out the cab and Jordan said, "What are you doing here?"

"You don't wanna see me? Fine then..."

"Trenice what's wrong with you?" he asked as he pulled me into a hug. "You know I wanna see you!"

"Can you come with me?"

"Sure." We both got in the cab and went to the Parkside Diner for brunch.

While we were at the table I explained what happened with Grandma.

"Well she's not stupid Trenice."

"Not you too – damn!"

"Calm down Trenice. I'm on your side, remember?"

"Yea sure," I said sarcastically.

"Why are you so mad anyway? If she knew the truth…"

"First of all she'll never know what really happened. Second of all we didn't break another bed, so I'm not lying when I tell her that!"

"Okay – okay," he laughed.

"What's so damn funny?"

"You are. Now hush up and kiss me silly," he said as he pulled me into a kiss…

"Mmm…"

"Isn't that better?"

"Much better."

"Ahem – are you ready to order?"

"Don't hate bitch," I said under my breath.

"Excuse me?"

"I said I'd like a western sandwich." Jordan looked at me giggling.

"And you?" she asked Jordan.

"I'll have pancakes and beef sausage."

"Would you like anything to drink?"

"Coffee for her, tea for me, and two glasses of water."

"Would you like lemon for your tea?"

"No – I'll take milk and sugar."

"I'll be back with your drinks."

"You are so bad," he said as she walked away.

"Fuck her," I laughed.

"What's gotten into you?"

"I dunno – I guess I'm frustrated 'cause of what happened earlier.

"Well the only way you can get away from that is if you move out," Jordan laughed. I looked at him without saying a word. When I sighed and put my hands under my chin he said, "Uh oh... what are you cooking up?" Just then the waitress came back with our drinks and put them on the table.

"Your food is coming right up."

"Thank you," we both said in unison.

While we were drinking our coffee and tea I said, "After we leave here I need to go see Dr. Campton."

"You do?"

"Yea – he's the one that has to take the cast off anyway."

"Oh I forgot about that... so are you gonna go back to your job when the cast comes off?"

"Probably – I like my job and the benefits are good so I don't see why not."

"Well I took this week off so I don't have to go back until Monday."

"What are you doing later today?" I asked as the waitress brought our food."

"Nothing – Why? You have something in mind?" He asked.

"You have to ask?"

When we left the diner we went straight to Dr. Campton's office. "I'm sorry but you don't have an appointment," the receptionist said.

"I know I don't (duh) but can you ask the doctor if he can squeeze me in?"

She sighed and mumbled under her breath, "I swear – this is sooo aggravating… hold on…Dr. Campton? Can you squeeze in Trenice Robertson? Ok… have a seat."

"Thank you." We didn't have to sit too long.

"C'mon in Trenice." When we got in the office he closed the door. "What happened this time Trenice?" Jordan and I looked at each other then at Dr. Campton.

"I fell Dr. Campton – but everyone else thinks we broke another bed."

"Well if I weren't a doctor I'd think that too."

"So you believe me?"

"Trenice I have your x-rays and I can tell by the break that you fell – you may have fallen out of a bed but you sure didn't break one," he laughed.

"Do you have a copy of the disability papers from my job?"

"No but we have papers here – we can just send them ours – as long as they're filled out properly you won't have a problem – do you still work at the Department of Social Services?"

"Yes."

"Ok – Jordan help Trenice up on the table so I can look at her cast." When I got up on the table he lifted up my leg. "See the x-ray there?"

"Yes."

"You broke your leg below the knee – the doctor put the cast on your leg over your knee so you can't bend it until it heals properly."

"Oh I see."

"He did a good job – we'll take care of everything as far as the paperwork – come back and see me in 6 weeks."

"Ok Dr. – thanks."

"Jordan?"

"Yes Dr.?"

"Make sure she's careful."

"Oh I will Dr."

When we got to the receptionist's desk I said sarcastically, "Excuse me – I need to **MAKE AN APPOINTMENT'** for 6 weeks from today." She wrote the appointment down on a card and slammed it on the counter so hard she broke one of her nails...

"**DAMMITT!**" she yelled.

"Buh bye!" I said as we left.

"Trenice that was mean," Jordan laughed.

"Fuck her – that's what she gets for being nasty," I laughed.

"So what did you have in mind?" he asked, changing the subject.

"Dessert."

"Oh I love dessert – should we stop at Carvel?" He asked.

"Very funny."

"Okay then – how 'bout the Trade Winds Hotel?"

"Now that's what I'm talking about!"

When we got into the room we pulled our clothes off with the quickness. "Let's do '**69**'!" I said.

"Ok – you get on top."

"OK!" I said as I climbed on top of him.

"Ouch!" he yelled as I kicked him in the head.

"I'm sorry," I laughed.

"This damn cast of yours is a pain in the ass!"

"I guess if we gonna be freaks we gotta suffer the consequences," I laughed as I slid down off of him and turned right side up on the bed to face him.

"I guess you're right," he said as he pulled me closer to him and we began exploring each other's mouths with our tongues while simultaneously exploring each other's bodies with our hands. Jordan was rock hard and I was soaking wet as he climbed on top of me and slid his cock inside. We started rocking back and forth and just as I was gettin' into it…"OUCH!"

"What's wrong?"

"This fuckin' cast is pinching my thigh!"

"Damn. Let me try again…This time I'll go slower…" Jordan said.

"Ohhhh… right there…"

"You like that?"

"Oh yea baby – that's it…I'm gonna cum…"

"Cum for me…Cum for me…"

"Oh   shit...it's   sooo   goodd...I'm cummin...I'm cummin..."

"I'm cummin with you... oh shit..."

"Yes... Yes..."

"Yes...Yes..."

The sweat was dripping from us both as we lie there kissing each other gently, licking each other's lips as our orgasms subsided..."MMMM...I could get used to this," Jordan said as he sucked on my bottom lip..."

"Nothing like a little dessert in the afternoon..." I said as I sucked his upper lip..."

"So what's stopping us?" he whispered in my ear while sucking on my ear lobe..."

"Who said anything about stopping?" I said as I kissed his neck...Jordan stopped and propped himself up on the pillow beside me.

"I'm serious Trenice."

"I was too..." I said as I started kissing his neck again..."

"Trenice look at me," he said as he took my face in his hands. He held my face and as we looked into each other's eyes he said, "I wanna do more of this. I wanna do this every day. I wanna go to sleep with you. I wanna wake up with you. I wanna come home to you."

"Wow," I said with tears in my eyes.

"Let's get our own place Trenice." I pulled him close and kissed him so hard I startled him.

"Damn girl – is that a yes?"

"Yes! Yes! Yes!"

When we left the hotel Jordan thought we were going home but he realized we weren't soon after we got in the cab. "Can you take us to 321 Main Street in White Plains?" I said to the driver.

"Ok Madam."

"Trenice what are you up to now?"

"You'll see…"

Chapter

45

When we got to Tyler's office Jordan was a little hesitant. "Trenice, are you sure about this?"

"Yes."

"Maybe we should leave well enough alone."

"Trust me."

"Ooookkkaaaayyyyy....."

"Hi Jordan, Trenice – Oh my God – what happened?" the receptionist asked as we walked into the waiting area.

"Oh I fell and broke my leg."

"Whew – for a second I thought you were suing another hotel," she laughed.

"So did everyone else," we laughed again.

"Do you need an appointment Trenice?" Tyler asked as he came out into the waiting area.

"Yes we do Tyler."

"Oh boy – c'mon into my office..." After we went into his office we closed the door and sat down.

"So what brings you both here?"

"Well, I fell and broke my leg while we were in Niagara Falls..."

"TRENICE!"

"Calm down honey...but that's not why we're here."

"Whew – glad to hear that at least.... go on..."

"Well, Jordan and I have decided to get a place of our own."

"Oh that's wonderful – congratulations!"

"Thank you."

"So when's the big day?"

"Oh we're not gettin' married."

"Oh sorry – I thought you were here to invite me to your wedding," he laughed.

"Oh you'll get an invitation to our wedding - don't worry – but that's not why we're here."

"Why are we here Trenice?" Jordan asked.

"Because we need Tyler to represent us."

"We do?"

"Yes."

"For what?"

"I'm tryin' to tell ya!"

"Okay – okay!"

"Go on Trenice," Tyler said.

"Well, as I said, we've decided to get our own place."

"Yes?"

"So since we have enough money for a down payment, we need you to represent us when we go to close on our new home."

"Trenice, that's a great idea and a great investment!"

"Trenice you never cease to amaze me, "Jordan said.

"So have you found anything yet?"

"No Tyler – we just decided to get our own place about an hour ago." Jordan and Tyler both bust out laughing.

"You don't waste any time do you?" Tyler asked.

"Not when it comes to something I want."

"Trenice are you sure we can afford a house right now? That's a big responsibility."

"Actually I was thinking more along the lines of a condo. They're more affordable and the monthly maintenance is cheaper than what we would pay in rent. Besides – unlike a co-op where you own shares in the building, with a condo, you own the apartment so you have more control."

"I see you've been doing your homework Trenice," Tyler laughed.

"Yes I have. "Well it would be my pleasure to represent you both."

"Okay – we'll keep in touch with you and let you know how everything's working out," I said as we left.

When we got outside Jordan asked, "How long have you been working on this?"

"I've been researching it since the day I met you," I said.

Jordan smiled, shook his head and asked, "So where to now?"

"Weichert Realtors." I said.

When we got to Weichert Realtors we signed up right away and I showed Jordan some of the properties I had been looking at. "Take this property for instance – they want $89,000 right?"

"Ok."

"It says the maintenance is $400 per month."

"Ok."

"It also says the taxes are $3,000 per year."

"Ok."

"So $80,000 over 30 years is $2,667 per year."

"Ok."

"So that's $222.25 per month plus $400 per month maintenance – that's $622.25 per month – without interest – I don't know how to factor that in."

"Ok."

"So $622.25 per month covers the mortgage and maintenance fees, $100 for the phone…"

"$100 for the phone?"

"I talk a lot remember?"

"Oh yea – go 'head...'"

"Now where was I...oh yea...$100 for the phone, $100 for Con Ed, $100 for cable, $200 for food...more or less..."

"Ok."

"That's $1,100 per month for everything right?"

"Yea... except for one thing."

"What's that?"

"Well you said $80,000 – this is $89,000."

"Well in that example we offer them $80,000."

"Oh I see..." Jordan laughed.

"But you still haven't calculated the interest over 30 years."

"I have an explanation for that too."

"I bet you do," he laughed, "Go 'head."

"Well, we still have plenty of money from our suit right?"

"Yea?"

"So if we wanted this property we offer $80,000 cash – who wouldn't take that?"

"Ok."

"So when we close, there's little or no cost – we pay our attorney, the seller pays Weichert Realtors out of the $80,000, and we don't have to buy homeowner's insurance 'cause it's built into our monthly maintenance."

"So we just cut that $1,100 a month down to $900."

"Exactly – and we have plenty of money left over to furnish the condo."

"Well what if we want a property that costs more? Like $120,000 or $200,000?"

"If we want a property for $200,000 we can pay cash for it too – then we'll only have the maintenance and expenses – it's still a win-win 'cause we won't have a mortgage – just think of it that way."

"You have a point."

Excerpt from:

How Far Are You Willing To Go? 2

"Bitch didn't I tell you mind your fuckin' business?" Once we heard the rumbling we knew what was going on...

"Get the fuck off me bitch!" Sissy yelled. Jordan and I were laughing with our hands over our mouths as we could tell that my mother was choking her...

"Trudy, get the fuck off me!" my mother yelled.

"Trenice come back..." Jordan tried to stop me but I was in the door already...

"Get the fuck off my mother!" I yelled as I snatched Aunt Trudy by the back of the shirt...

"Bitch please," Aunt Trudy said as she pushed me to the floor...

"Bang!"

Secrets Tree

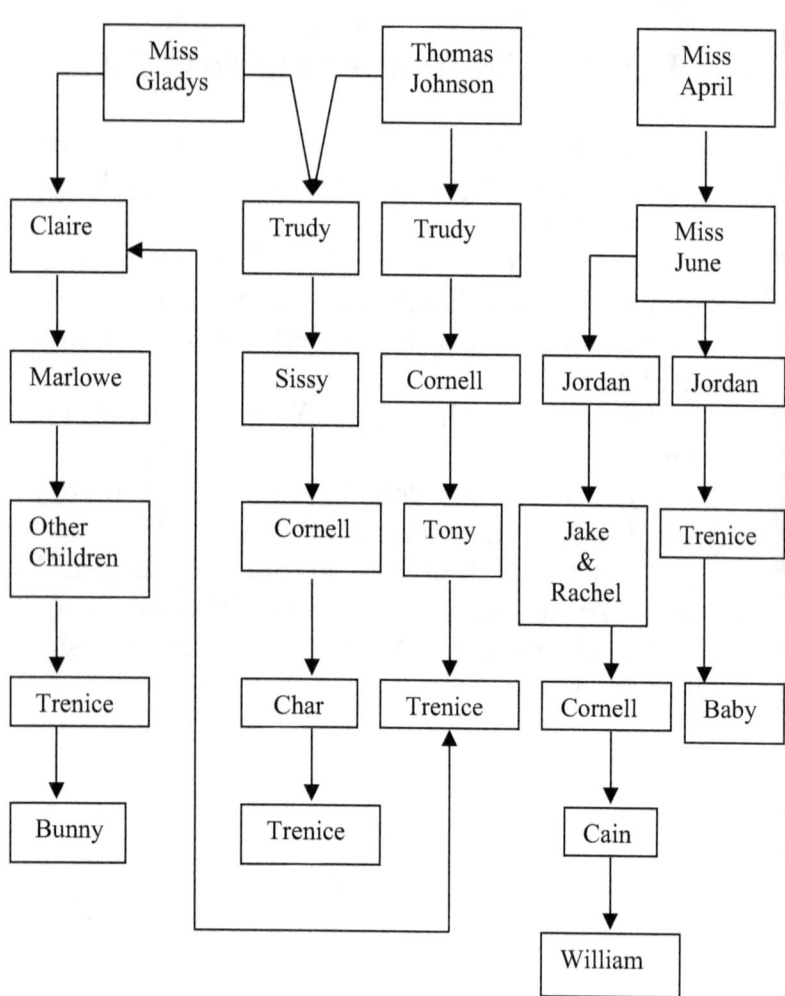

<u>Secrets Tree</u>

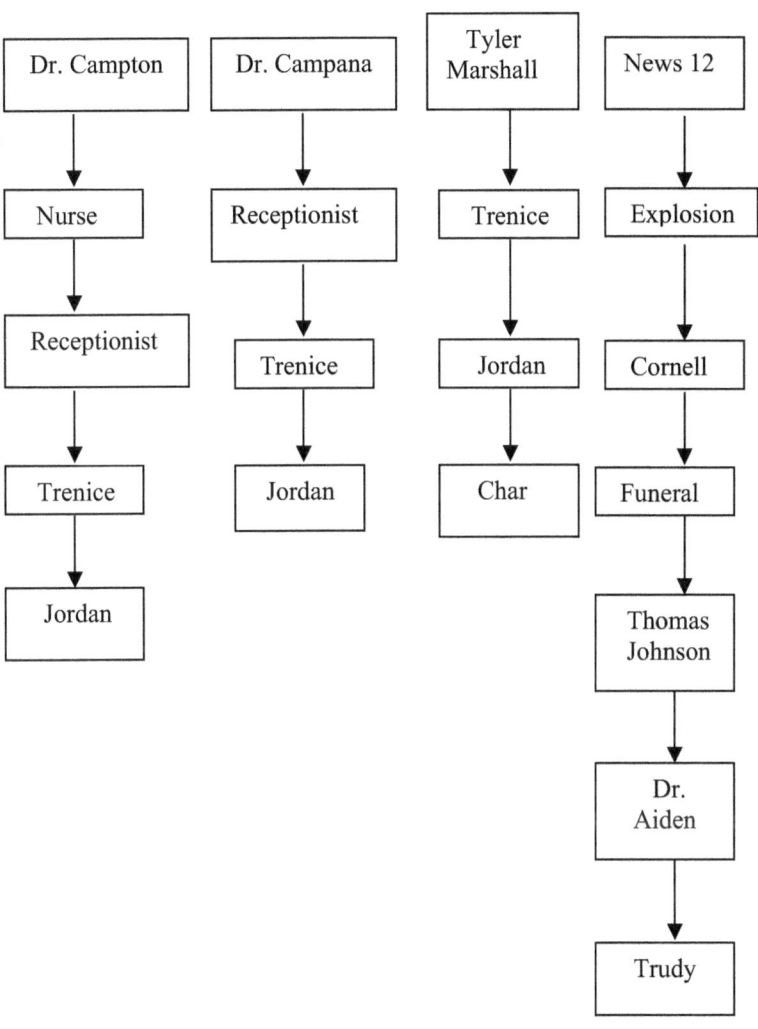

"You are calling your dates, functions now?"

"No," Mason stood up, "It's actually a get together at the Carr's place. I am late."

"They are always having parties." Elsa snorted, "are you going as Yara's date?"

Mason raised an eyebrow. "Would that bother you?"

"No," Elsa got up too and walked toward the door.

A ghost of a smile crossed Mason's face, and she stopped. "You smiled!"

"I smile all the time," Mason said, turning serious again.

"No, you don't. You are not programmed to smile."

"So, you still think I am an android?" Mason chuckled. "I thought you had moved on from that theory when you were fifteen. I think the following year, I was an alien."

"A Vulcan, filled with logic and no emotion," Elsa muttered. "I can't believe you remembered that."

"I remember everything, Elsa." Mason touched the down button for the elevator and turned to look at her. "Every single detail about everything, especially four years ago, when you threw yourself at me. I could have had you then." Elsa inhaled raggedly and avoided looking at him.

"But I declare a truce," Mason said when they got in the elevator together. "I will not bring up the past, what happened is our secret."